CONTRAILS

A Novel

Airline Flying in Eastern Europe
before the "Wall" Came Down

BILL SIREN

iUniverse, Inc.
Bloomington

Contrails

A Novel: Airline Flying in Eastern Europe before the "Wall" Came Down

iUniverse books may be ordered through booksellers or by contacting:

iUniverse
1663 Liberty Drive
Bloomington, IN 47403
www.iuniverse.com
1-800-Authors (1-800-288-4677)

ISBN: 978-1-4759-6600-8 (s)
ISBN: 978-1-4759-6603-9 (e)
ISBN: 978-1-4759-6602-2 (hc)

Library of Congress Control Number: 2012923077

Printed in the United States of America

iUniverse rev. date: 1/30/2013

For my wife, Allison, my copilot through life's flight—although we often changed seats. I am grateful for her forbearance with my vivid imagination. To my children, who complete my life, and to my grandchildren, who are the joy of my life. No person could ask for more.

High Flight

Oh, I have slipped the surly bonds of Earth
And danced the skies on laughter-silvered wings;
…I've trod…The sanctity of space…
… and touched the face of God

—John Gillespie Magee, Jr.

Contents

PREFACE

FLYING IS A NOBLE endeavor. Although powered flight is less than two centuries old, it has produced countless innovations and pioneers and has tested the human spirit's limits. For over twenty thousand years, civilized man functioned in two dimensions and traveled no faster than the speed of a horse. More recently, however, man has explored three-dimensional realms under the sea, in the air, and in outer space. In the nineteenth century, we developed more sophisticated means with the coming of the industrial age and advances in technology—steam, electric, electronic, telephonic, and so forth.

This book is about the narrower field of airline flying—specific in the scientific area but profound in the means of human transportation. This historical fiction is my attempt to portray what being a pilot is all about—what the career entails, a realistic presentation of the profession, and the lives its practitioners lead with colleagues and the public. The pervading theme herein, however, is the confluence of morality and mortality.

Contrails, or vapor trails, are long, thin artificial clouds that sometimes form behind aircraft when certain pressure and temperature conditions cause exhaust particles and water vapor to combine. They are more or less an airplane's signature in the sky, so Contrails seemed to be an apt name for an airline and for a book on aviation.

Flyers take to the skies in fixed-wing, rotary-wing, lighter-than-air, and glider aircraft. They fly hang gliders, seaplanes, parasails, remote-controlled aircraft, spaceships, and even chairs attached to lawnmower engines and kites. Pilots take the forms of true professionals, novices, drunks, clowns, and showmen who sometimes push their aircraft outside its operating envelope. There are old pilots and bold pilots, but few old, bold pilots.

Jokes, gaffes, and bon mots about aviation circle the world at faster than Mach 1, the speed of sound. Especially poignant tales hold in a low-earth orbit, waiting to be pinged down to awaiting ears. Such stories, oral or printed, true or fictional, are part of the aviation culture and necessitate no attribution.

Those who want to travel from point A to point B without hassle—if that's possible—may have no interest in what goes on in cockpits and will perhaps skim the few technical issues about aviation I present. I hope, nevertheless, they find the underlying narrative interesting.

Many others, however, want to know more about aviation technology and pilot procedures; I offer some of these issues to them and hope they find my presentation engaging.

This portrayal includes mostly authentic events, but the reader will find many anecdotes that are true or at least have their place in aviation lore. Other events and stories here are in the minds and hearts of professional aviators. I experienced many of the situations in this work, but the interpersonal relationships of an amorous nature portrayed in this book are imaginary.

Other relationships herein are products of my imagination

or fictitious depictions of real events, except for my experiences in the navy. The setting for this tale, at least for the time involving airline flying, is the late 1980s. Around that time, the term "flight attendant" was replacing the age-old "stewardess," but many old-timers had a little trouble with that, so both will appear. Also during that time, because relatively few pilots in military and airline cockpits were female, this work refers only to male pilots.

I relied on my logbooks, old flight manuals, conversations with friends, and memories forever imprinted in my mind in writing this book. I've taken some liberties with aeronautical innovations and the timing of some events all for the sake of interest. The lyrics to songs, hymns, or poems list the lyricists or origins of the songs. I've given just the beginnings of the works and cut some to four lines. "High Flight," by John Gillespie Jr., is a poignant paean to aviators who revel in the thrill of freedom the skies offer and who have had the chance to feel the touch of their Creator. All the words to these works are on the Internet; they all seem apropos to the story.

Any relationships in this book that deal with individuals or actual organizations, whether extant or defunct, are certainly recreations of reality or my interpretations of authentic happenings. Except those of a historical nature, all names are fictitious. I take the blame for any errors in aeronautical terms or explanations.

CONTRAILS

CHAPTER ONE

Off we go into the wild blue yonder,
Climbing high into the sun;
Here they come zooming to meet our thunder,
At 'em boys, Give 'er the gun!

—The Air Force Hymn

IT WAS RYAN LASSETER'S turn to fly the Moscow-to-Leningrad leg, as the captain had flown the Heathrow-to-Moscow leg to the *Sheremetyevo* Airport. The talking pilot and the flying pilot rotate on each leg of daily flights. The former reads the checklists, talks to controllers, gives altitude warnings, and monitors safety. The flying pilot handles the controls (except for taxiing, when the left-seat pilot has control of nose-wheel steering) and talks to the passengers at the captain's discretion. Before descending from cruise altitude, the pilot at the controls briefs the other pilot on the approach plate that depicts headings, altitudes, obstructions, minimum altitudes, and so forth for the final phase of the flight. The approach plate is a piece of paper, about five and a half inches by eight and a half inches, that depicts instrument approaches to runways at various airports. Pilots carry hundreds of them in a binder.

Before being recalled by Contrails, Ryan had served in the

navy and had seen various duty stations as his rank increased during his layoff. His military duties had kept him away from the cockpit for over seven years. His last flying had been in the navy in P-3 aircraft. He went through the training syllabus easily for the Boeing 727, a three-engine aircraft with the engines in the aft empennage, or tail. His training had involved ground-school training and an in-flight checkout.

Ryan had only recently returned to Contrails World Airways after a lengthy furlough—an experience many airline pilots endure as air carriers go through hiring and layoff cycles, recession and growth, expansion and contraction—all dependent on the economy, terrorism, new equipment, and the type of airplanes the company operates. Some airplanes require a three-man crew while others need a two-man crew; some very long flights require relief crews.

After training, he was assigned as a first officer, or copilot, in Berlin; this was when the Cold War was being waged and the Berlin Wall was standing. After he arrived in Berlin, the European domicile for Contrails, he went through a five-day route check by a senior pilot who evaluated and educated pilots about flying in Europe as opposed to flying in the United States. And there were many differences—variations on when to set altimeter settings for local pressure conditions and when to transition to settings for standard sea-level pressure. All this was needed to ensure vertical separation among the many airplanes occupying the skies.

His route check went well. One of his first trips took him from Frankfurt to London. He was flying the 727, the last of the medium-sized aircraft to have a three-man crew. He was a little nervous as he tried to get used to the procedures. Taking off from Frankfurt, he followed the standard instrument departure plate and climbed to thirty-one thousand feet. He followed his en route chart he kept handy for the flight to Heathrow, which was to take an hour and fifteen minutes. Just before he began his descent into Heathrow, the captain asked him to say a few words to the passengers. He made a few notes and, since the flight engineer had already obtained the weather in London, he made a standard spiel about their altitude and the weather, and he included the standard takeoff phrase, "Sit back, relax, and enjoy the flight," forgetting they were landing at that point. It was his first time making the announcement, so on top of it all, his voice was a little shaky. He went back to studying the approach plate because he'd heard things happened fast as you approach Heathrow, and the controllers expected prompt compliance with instructions. He was busier than the proverbial one-armed paperhanger. A flight attendant brought breakfast for all three in the cockpit, delicious-looking French toast and bacon. The two pilots didn't normally eat at the same time, but since it was a short flight, they were willing to make an exception. Ryan, however, just didn't feel comfortable eating with so much going on, so he declined the meal, knowing he would soon be starting the descent. He briefed the pilot on the approach and began the standard terminal area route procedure. Things did happen fast, and the captain talked him politely through a couple of items. But it went rather well, and they landed without any problems. It proved to be an excellent introduction to the way most of his short flights would go.

Ryan knew the two basic techniques to put a 727 on the ground. He could "roll" the aircraft onto the runway, a technique that required pushing the yoke forward, which gently lifted the landing gear relative to the runway as the aircraft kept descending. Or he could pull back on the yoke, which reduced the rate of descent but caused the gear to rotate downward, possibly causing a hard landing. Nevertheless, Ryan found the latter way preferable since it was more in tune with the way he had landed multiengine aircraft in the navy. He knew that contrary to popular belief, a three-point-landing was not perfect for aircraft with nose wheels. With a slight misjudgment, the nose gear could hit first, causing it to collapse, or if it didn't collapse, the landing would be porpoise-like.

Ryan knew the drill: the aerodynamic center of his plane was the fulcrum around which pitching occurred. A little physics showed that for a body to be in equilibrium, all forces and moments had to balance. In flight, at least in most conventional aircraft, the CG, or center of gravity, was forward of the aerodynamic center and provided a downward force. The center of lift (the lift created by the entire aircraft—mainly the wings) was aft of the CG. That meant that the aft horizontal stabilizer, with a long moment arm, provided a downward force for equilibrium.

Even though he had always excelled in military aviation, Ryan had felt a little uncomfortable during his approach to Leningrad's *Pulkovo* Airport on this last leg. It was winter, and the skies were dark as ebony, except for the snowfall. Snow drifted on the runway, and a slight crosswind complicated the landing. One additional complication was that the altimeter settings for the approach had been based on actual airport pressure rather than sea level pressure. On landing, therefore, the altimeter would show zero altitude. In addition, all altitude assignments and minimums were based on meters rather than feet, so the pilot had to add a conversion chart to his scan pattern, all the elements he had to refer to visually. The pilots had changed from the foot-pound system to the metric system over Riga, Latvia. In areas outside the Eastern Bloc, the altimeter showed height above sea level, and the approach chart showed the airport's height above sea level. On landing, therefore, the altimeter showed the airport's actual height above sea level. This was confusing for pilots in training, but after they did it a few times, it got to be second nature. The problem was the split second it took to convert from meters to feet, and in any challenging approach, every second counted. The most dangerous parts of any flight were the takeoff and the landing. Setting down in snow and ice at night increased the peril exponentially, but airline pilots were well trained for this.

Earlier, in Berlin (pronounced BEAR-lin), Ryan had introduced himself to the captain at the operations desk where they filed the flight plan, checked the weather, and filled out the "bug sheet"—the takeoff thrust settings and flap settings for the airport's variable meteorological conditions and fixed runway length. It also showed the runway speed beyond which pilots could not abort with a lost engine because of the lack of remaining runway. The bug sheet went on the middle console between the pilots, right by the thrust levers.

The cockpit crew had met up in operations at the required time, forty-five minutes before pushback, and Ryan introduced himself to the captain. "I'm Ryan Lasseter. I'll be flying with you." The four-striper responded, "I'm Simon Razocovik. You can call me Captain Whacko."

Ryan considered that strange. He also thought it strange that while they had had a German cabin flight crew from Berlin for the one-hour flight to Frankfurt, the turnaround in Frankfurt heading for Moscow included a completely Polish flight attendant crew. He learned it was the norm, the policy, when they flew to an airport behind the Iron Curtain. He didn't meet the women until they boarded the aircraft, and they were indeed beautiful. In fact, Contrails at the time had a strict hiring policy for flight attendants. They had to be under thirty, under 130 pounds, speak English as well as another language, and, well, be impressive in appearance. Ryan briefly met some of the women while getting coffee in the first-class galley, and their first names all seemed to end in vowels. Their last names, which the flight engineer had to enter into the flight log, were largely unpronounceable. The engineer remarked at one point that he could manage only one name, so the purser had to write them all out.

Ryan was struck by one in particular—a gorgeous, dark-haired beauty who seemed out of place in the group of four, but he and the captain settled into their seats, got out their charts, and engaged in small talk since they had ten minutes before they'd have to get serious. Ryan asked, "Captain Whacko, huh? May I ask the origin of that?"

Cracker crumbs, of all things, shot out like ballistic missiles from the captain's mouth along with his words. "Well, I fly by the book, young man, although you're not so young, but this is just a job, and we have to enjoy the time we have, and there's fun to be found everywhere. You're new to Berlin, so let me brief you on the differences between our operations here and in the States. We're like a squadron, which you probably know from your navy days. We look out for each other and our dependents in Berlin. If, for example, your wife wants to accompany you on a trip to London, we put her onboard even if the flight's full. We'll put her in the empty flight attendant's seat, in the cockpit in an empty seat, or in the loo—whatever it takes. If she's in the loo on takeoff, she'll occupy one of the attendants' jump seats once we're airborne. Got it?"

"Yes sir. Anything else I should know?" Ryan asked.

"Do you know the difference between heaven and hell in Europe?" the captain asked.

"No."

"Heaven in Europe is when the cooks are French, the lovers Italian, the mechanics German, the police British, and the whole show's run by the Swiss. Hell over here is when the cooks are British, the lovers are Swiss, the mechanics French, the police German, and the whole thing's run by the Italians."

Ryan guffawed—the whole stereotype thing. Anyhow, Simon set the tone for the trip, and Ryan found him loose and easy to fly with. He soon learned that some airlines used unique call signs, telephony (ta-LEF-a-nee), rather than company names. For example, British Airways used "Speedbird" in its call sign. "Speedbird 101" would mean British Airways flight 101. Pan Am used "Clipper," Aer Lingus used "Shamrock," America West was "Cactus," South African Airways used "Springbok," and so forth. Other airlines just used the company name. Ryan thought "Continental" was an awkward call sign as it contained four syllables, and TWA's was difficult to use without using the silly *dub-ya* for the *w*. A lot of folks thought the telephony "Vapor" or "Vortex" would have worked well for Contrails, but "Contrails" prevailed since it had been a legacy carrier over the years.

Ryan had another learning experience. In Europe, some airports went by their ethnic rather than their English names, so the Munich tower was *Munchen* tower, the Prague approach was *Praha* approach, the Athens control was *Athena* control, the Rome approach was *Roma* approach, and so forth. In Germany, certain idioms were used. In Bavaria, especially in Munich, or *Munchen,* the phrase *Gross Gott* was common. It loosely meant "Go with God" or "Aloha" or maybe "*Ciao.*" So after takeoff, when the tower said "Contrails 126 switch to departure on 122.4," the response would be "126 switching to 122.4, *Gross Gott.*" Another example involved the common word for "bye-bye," *tschuss,* in Hamburg. The pilot would say something like, "Contrails 138 switching to 124.2, *tschuss.*" Ryan learned that while these words and phrases weren't obligatory, they soon became second nature.

On the final approach to runway ten right at Leningrad's *Pulkovo* Airport during that flight, the localizer course bar, which indicated alignment with the runway, was moving right to left and left to right at a steady rate, but it generally averaged on centerline. The course bar seemed much more sensitive than usual, but Ryan attributed this to inferior Russian landing approach systems. The Russian controllers, although ostensibly English speakers, were tough to understand. Ryan and Whacko managed to discern the proper runway, got clearance to land, and checked the altimeter setting and the wind, which was quartering from the left of the aircraft at fifteen miles per hour. This meant Ryan had to "crab," or head the plane slightly left of the runway centerline, to stay on course. Just prior to touchdown, he'd have to lower the left wing and apply a little right rudder to avoid landing with lateral stress on the gear.

The sparkling snowflakes illuminated by the landing lights showed up as large as snowballs. Ryan asked for the landing gear to be lowered, and Whacko said, "Yes, the undercarriage makes for a smoother touchdown. Not to mention it makes the taxiing infinitely easier." Ryan didn't need any humor, however. He was tense. He wiped his palms on his pants. He could see the approach lights barely above minimums; he kept scanning for airspeed, altitude, and lineup. For altitude monitoring when the runway was in sight, he checked the VASI, the visual approach slope indicator, for altitude monitoring—two banks of lights separated by a few dozen meters to the left of the runway and near the approach end. Each light's lens was divided horizontally, with white showing on top and red on bottom. They provided the pilot with a three-degree descent rate. If Ryan saw one set as white and the second as red, he'd know he had the aircraft on the correct glide slope. Red over red would mean he was too low, while white over white meant too high. Ryan followed the VASI after breaking clear of the ceiling, put the landing correction in, and gently flared the airplane as he was near actual landing. To his surprise, they touched down with the soft feet of a dove—his best landing ever in a 727. As he gently braked and the spoilers went up to dump the lift, which put the full aircraft weight on the gear, the plane slowed, and he began to hear applause from the cabin. As they taxied in, Ryan's nerves relaxed, but he again had to wipe his hands on his pants.

At the Moscow one-hour turnaround earlier, when the passengers disembarked, a huge Russian guard with a grey greatcoat and a fur hat with flaps buttoned over the head had entered the aircraft. Before the captain went into operations to file the paperwork and the engineer left the plane for a walk-around inspection, they handed their passports to the guard. Ryan had stayed aboard with the flight attendants to tend to some paperwork. The guard approached Ryan and handed him a set of Russian wings. Ryan was stunned by the act of apparent goodwill. The guard smiled at him and said "*Da.*" Ryan was flabbergasted and thought briefly about giving him the wings off his own uniform but thought they were too valuable, so he handed the guard a deck of Contrails playing cards. The guard said "*Spasiba*" and smiled again. Ryan realized these folks were real people, not mortal enemies.

They left Moscow for Leningrad, where customs was a real experience. All the flight crewmembers except for Ryan had been to Russia before, and they all required just a few minutes of questioning before being waved in. When Ryan handed over his passport at the window, the agent, who had a buzz-cut hair style, a pockmarked face, and an angry demeanor, told him to wait. He was gone about ten minutes. When he came back, he stared at Ryan and his passport, asked some perfunctory questions, and told him to wait some more. It took ten more minutes before he cleared Ryan with a dismissive wave of the hand. The agent never mentioned it, but Ryan realized since he had left the United States military only a couple of months earlier, he was surely in the Russian computer system. The wait probably entailed checking various databases to ascertain whether he was involved in any special projects with people on which they had dossiers. Ryan's last few jobs in the navy had involved budgetary issues, but he had access to and often read classified documents because he had top-secret clearance.

The crewmembers were curious about what had happened, but he left them clueless. The crew had had dinner during the flight, and the layover made for a rather short night, so Ryan hadn't had a real chance to interact with the rest of the crew. The women seemed to huddle during the downtimes and while riding on the flight-crew shuttle.

The crew usually stayed at three- or four-star hotels, Hiltons, Sheratons, or InterContinentals. Leningrad made no room for capitalistic ventures, so they stayed at one of the best hotels in the city. It seemed nice judging from the lobby—a lot of chandeliers, clerks, and cleanliness. The cockpit crew all had private rooms, but the stews had to double up. After Ryan checked in, a female clerk escorted him to his room. He noticed his hand was shaking when he registered. Was he still nervous from that approach? He'd never experienced this before, but he shook it off as a remnant of the customs ordeal and for being in the Soviet Union for the first time. He tried to make small talk with his guide, but her demeanor was stoic—he felt she had the impression the KGB was everywhere. As he walked to his room, he saw men lying on the hallways—dead or drunk. He asked the guide about this but got no response.

Ryan got to his room, which was clean, but then he noticed a single bed. He turned on the TV, which had only two channels, both in black and white—a ping-pong tournament and a ballet. The bathroom had what Americans would call tea towels for bath towels and waxed paper for toilet tissue. Ryan changed and met the captain in the basement bar. The captain had a fair amount of rubles with him—experienced crewmembers always carried various foreign currencies with them. This necessitated a shoulder bag—a place to carry passports, currencies, guides, and so forth. Some ridiculed this as part of a rather effeminate accessory, but, hey, whatever worked was their attitude. When Ryan ordered a Russian beer, the barkeep looked at him as though he should have ordered vodka. The drink came, along with a request in poor English, "Three dollars, please." Ryan said he had rubles, but the bartender repeated "Three dollars." He paid as the captain said, "You'll find in Eastern Europe they love to deal in only hard currency—dollars, pounds, or marks." Lesson learned.

After a few beers, which were surprisingly good, he bade the captain good night. He said, "Yes, we can't stay up with the owls and fly with the eagles." He asked the captain about the bodies in the hallways and learned that on Friday nights Finns came by train to Leningrad to get drunk because alcohol was so much cheaper in Russia. They would stay drunk until Sunday and go home. They would simply find a hotel in which to pass out, and the management seemed to tolerate it to get their business.

Thus began one of the many adventures Ryan experienced with Contrails in Europe.

Chapter Two

Far away places with strange sounding names
Far away over the sea
Those far away places with the strange sounding names are
Calling

—Joan Whitney, Alex Kramer

RYAN AND HIS WIFE, Lexi, had settled into a small, one-bedroom apartment on *Eislebener Strasse* (ize-LEEB-ner strassa), just three blocks from the main shopping avenue in Berlin—the *Kurfurstendamm*, or *KuDam*. His wife's first name was actually Alexsandra, from which various nicknames could be made; she was a tall, blue-eyed blonde and very athletic. They had a home in San Diego and a good although fairly new marriage.

Lexi Logan was Ryan's second wife—they had been married about four years when Ryan joined Contrails for the second time. His first wife, Claire Glenn, was a real beauty and was, he had thought for a long time, absolutely perfect for him—no one could ever surpass her in his mind. They had been voted high school king and queen of their senior dance, got married, and had two children, Pam and Todd. They were intellectual equals, and she was full of kindness and fun. But she was no pushover when challenged. When pushed, she would push back harder. When Ryan served at the Pentagon for six years, Claire got a business degree at George Mason University and obtained a job with a clothing designer and manufacturer. She loved the job and often spent weekends at work. She also took some courses in fashion design and began working with a clothing company that specialized in women's sportswear. Claire had a responsible position that included design and marketing. Ryan knew all along he would return to Contrails someday since his seniority was protected, and he had no desire to be in the running for becoming an admiral, even though he had the qualifications to be competitive for that selection. He had no desire to play politics—his interests were in flying, engineering, and business. But he knew he would have to make one more military move before he would be recalled to the airline. Claire loved her work but seemingly was no longer really in love with Ryan; she was adamant about not moving.

The couple gradually grew out of love but remained friends and eventually got a divorce. Ryan's soul was fractured by the split, for although the relationship was strained, he was blindsided by the request for a divorce. He told Claire, "I tried to be a good husband. I brought you flowers. I cooked and helped with the kids' homework. We did things together—we traveled."

"It was the lack of tenderness, Ryan. You were rational and objective but detached. You were a Dr. Spock from *Star Trek*. I needed love."

"I love you, but I hope you find what you want. You knew what I was like early on. People don't really change much. The kids love us both—we'll see what happens, Claire."

"It's not a contest—it's life."

"Think back, Claire, to high school and college. What were you looking for? Turn back the clock, do it over, but forget about me. I'll love you and treasure all the good times. I'll move on and try to forget whatever deters me from a good future."

Their children were attending college, which simplified things somewhat. Claire got about half their net worth, including the house in Springfield, Virginia, but no alimony. Ryan would pay for their children's college, which wasn't that big a burden since Ryan was paying in-state tuition for them. Ryan's new orders would take him to San Diego, where he would work as a comptroller for the commander of Naval Aviation Forces in the Pacific.

Ryan had met Lexi at the Springfield, Virginia country club just before his move to California. They'd been paired in a mixed foursome golf tournament and had hit it off. The other twosome was Dale and Betty. Dale asked, "Do you want to hear a golf joke?"

Ryan and Lexi were open to that.

"A husband and wife were lying in bed, and the wife asked the husband if he would remarry if she died. He said, 'Well, you know I like people and I'd be lonely, so I probably would marry someone else.'

"'Well, would she live in this house?'

"'It's a big house, fully paid for, so I suppose she'd live here.'

"'Would she sleep in this bed?'

"'It's a king-size bed,' the husband said, 'the right degree of firmness, fairly new, so yes, I guess she'd sleep in this bed.'

"'Would she use my golf clubs?'

"'No, she's left-handed.'"

Ryan and Lexi laughed. Ryan said, "Lexi, I'm glad you're right handed."

The four became good friends and played a lot of golf, and Ryan and Lexi also played tennis at the club. The relationship grew stronger. She was gregarious and pretty—a pert blonde well-liked by all and readily accepted into Ryan's circle of friends. They married, and she accompanied him on his final tour of duty in the navy to San Diego. Lexi's sister Camille lived in Williamsburg, Virginia; she had leukemia, and Lexi often visited her. Another sister, Marlie, married to a navy SEAL, lived in Norfolk, Virginia and visited Camille often since she was less than a half-day drive away.

After two years in San Diego, Ryan finished his final six months of military obligation, retired, and was recalled by Contrails for a first officer position in Berlin. Off they went for the adventure in Europe.

Ryan was in an unusual situation. A navy tour, an airline tour, another navy tour followed by retirement from the service, and then a position again with the airline. He knew only a handful of others who had experienced the wonderful fulfillment of two careers.

Lexi had a teaching credential, which she was using when the two met. They had the same values and dreams. She was smart and nice to everyone. He couldn't imagine his new life without her. He had been terribly lonely after his divorce, and she made him a stronger person. Though Ryan loved her, he thought now and then it might have been a rebound marriage. It wasn't that he hadn't committed his total life to her, but, being a rational man, he wondered whether a marriage so soon after a divorce had been some kind of a temporary fix. Should he have waited longer before such a commitment? He knew that flying in Europe would bring a whole world of complications and that Lexi would have to fly to America often. One plus was that they would be constantly traveling in Europe.

Being based in Berlin was strictly voluntary. Since most pilots had a home and family in America, a foreign station could involve separation for weeks at a time. Because the Berlin base was two hundred miles behind the Iron Curtain, most flights always departed westward, through one of three air corridors, below ten thousand feet until they were in West German airspace. They would often be accompanied by a MIG fighter and see tank maneuvers on the ground near Fulda, near the border with West Germany. Approaches to Berlin also took one of the air corridors, and landings were virtually always made to the west. On clear days, in VMC, visual meteorological conditions, they would fly around a twelve-hundred-foot TV tower in Alexanderplatz—the heart of East Berlin. They would keep the tower off their left wing as they made their approach to final. They could often see the hundred-mile-long Berlin Wall as it wound around the western part of the city like an ugly scar. The Wall had gone up in 1961 to keep easterners out of West Berlin; the city was divided, the eastern part under the aegis of the Red Army. Although over forty years had passed since the end of World War II, bombed-out buildings were still there, along with Soviet-style drab, concrete high-rises.

Ryan knew a lot of the history of the area. In 1945, after victory in Europe, the conquering allies had met in Potsdam to decide the postwar makeup of the continent. Berlin was divided into four sectors, three of which would be under the control of Britain, France, and the United States and made up the city's western half, and the Soviets controlled the eastern half. In 1948, all Germany was divided roughly in half. West Germany became the Federal Republic of Germany, and its currency was the deutschmark. East Germany became the German Democratic Republic with the reichsmark as the currency. Soviet premier Nikita Khrushchev wanted Berlin to be a free city, but thousands of East Germans started pouring into West Berlin. When Khrushchev blockaded the city, the allies began airlifting supplies necessary for survival. By 1961, the Soviets were losing control of East Germany, and Berlin became divided physically by barbed wire at first and later by concrete, dog runs, and guard stations.

Soon after, America become mired in Vietnam, and little attention was given to West Berlin, although President Kennedy visited the city in June, 1963 and declared *"Ich bin ein Berliner,"* "I am a Berliner," thus securing the friendship between the FRG and America.

Ryan learned firsthand that in the winter, Berlin—indeed much of northern Europe—had poor visibility as far as landings were concerned. Pilots frequently couldn't catch a glimpse of the runway until they were just one hundred feet above the ground or about a quarter of a mile away. But the Berlin operation had its advantages. Things were loosely run, which is not to say unprofessional, and there was close camaraderie. Contrails gave its Berlin-based cockpit crewmembers a foreign-station allowance, a tidy sum. In addition, Berlin, probably in long-standing gratitude for America's role in the Berlin airlift following the Berlin blockade of 1948–49, gave the pilots a "Berlin Bonus"—another tidy sum of marks deposited directly into crewmembers' Berliner Bank accounts. Along with the chance to see much of Europe, these incentives made the station an enjoyable experience.

Ryan had an interesting time filing his income tax with H&R Block in West Berlin in 1988. He had military active duty as well as retirement income, Contrails income, a moving allowance, uniform and flight equipment deductions, per diem allowances, German income tax, and a Berlin bonus in marks. The Block agent was perplexed, and Ryan ended up getting audited, but he sailed through it, probably because the IRS agent also was confused.

Ryan tried to compress his flying into about twenty days a month and then enjoy about ten days off. One month he would pack in his work at the beginning of the month, and the next month he would fly mostly in the latter part of the month. This usually gave him about fifteen days in California or Virginia, as necessity would have it, every other month or so. He and Lexi always flew home from Frankfurt nonstop to Los Angeles or Washington, DC—about a fourteen- or a ten-hour flight. They always flew first class, which cost employees about $25 each, and they had to wear a coat and tie or appropriate dress. First class in Contrails was special—all-you-could drink champagne, caviar, and prime rib carved by the seat. It made the time go by easily.

Ryan had good seniority in Berlin, and everything about being an airline pilot was based on seniority—where you were based, what equipment you flew, the routes you flew, and promotions. Because seniority was based strictly on one's hiring date and since Ryan had been in the military when Contrails recalled him, his seniority had been protected by law when he had military obligations due to promotions, change of duty stations, or advanced schooling. He therefore could bid the routes and dates he wanted to fly and be fairly sure of getting close to what he asked for. Lexi went with him on most of his flights on a space-available basis, but at times she flew to Dulles Airport in DC and drove to Williamsburg to be with Camille.

Ryan flew patterns that varied from one to six days. A one-day pattern might be two round trips from Berlin to Hamburg. A six-day pattern could include a deadhead flight to Paris for an overnight, a nonstop to Tel Aviv the next day, and another overnight before going back to Paris, followed by a repetition of the first three days. The entire month involved about seventeen days of duty.

Ryan found Tel Aviv to be a wonderful layover city. His captain told him to get some shekels in the hotel lobby because he knew a nice restaurant. Lexi was with him on that trip, and they left their beautiful hotel on the shores of the Mediterranean and walked through old town Tel Aviv and through the very old city of Jaffa, known in the Bible as Joppa—the city from which Noah launched his ark. The streets were narrow and some buildings were crumbling, but the whole scene was fascinating. They arrived at a small, unassuming restaurant after about a two-mile stroll. The captain said, "I hope you like lamb—that's all they serve here." They had lamb meatballs, lamb chops, lamb kabobs, and other delicacies until they were wonderfully stuffed.

Generally, on layover flights away from Berlin, if they arrived at their hotel around dinnertime, the whole crew would go out to dinner. If they arrived late, they would have dinner on the aircraft. In those cases, after the cockpit crew had checked in at the hotel, they would head to a spot or lounge in the bar (in Germany, this was called a *stube*—a warm, cozy place) and perhaps have some goulash and a beer or two. Frankfurt was the most common layover; a late arrival there meant a stay at the airport InterContinental, but an early arrival meant a room at the downtown InterContinental. At the downtown hotel, crews would usually go to a favorite restaurant and haunt for Contrails crews, The Gas Station, actually *Baseler Eck*, but it was by a gas station about three blocks from the hotel. They would frequently meet crews that had flown in on 747s on transatlantic flights, or Airbus crews, or 727 folks, and the food was great, including *schweinshaxe*, pig's knuckle boiled and then broiled until the skin was crisp—a wonderful pork delight.

As Ryan sat at the table enjoying beer, pork, and the camaraderie one night, he couldn't help but notice a woman sitting with another flight crew about fifteen feet away. She was striking in appearance—a raven-haired beauty with a warm smile. Her graceful demeanor and easy air made Ryan think she was a clone of Lexi, just with a different hair color. Ryan wondered who she was. A flight attendant for sure, but did she fly out of Berlin? He knew he had seen her before, but where? Her group left before Ryan's, and he smiled and said hello as she passed by. She returned the smile and replied, "*Guten Tag.*" *That was nice*, he thought. *I wonder if I'll fly with her someday.*

Free days in Berlin involved exploring the city, and there was much to see. Ryan's and Lexi's second-story flat was furnished in a midcentury style—tasseled lampshades and such—but they spruced it up with modern occasional pieces. They slept with featherdeckers on the bed—goose-down quilts—which kept them comfortable in all seasons. The Brandenburg Gate was about two miles from their apartment and next to the Wall. They could see into East Berlin from a platform by the Wall, including no-man's land—a barren strip about one hundred yards deep and patrolled by guard dogs. They could go to the Wall by crossing a bridge over the river Spree, where anyone trying to swim to freedom would be shot. They would stroll the KuDam, spend a day at Lake Wannsee, enjoy a lunch in Grunewald forest, or visit the famous zoo at the Tiergarten. They loved to visit the Ka De We department store, only three blocks from their apartment. It was the largest department store in continental Europe, much like Harrods in London, a fabulous bazaar where everything was beautifully displayed. The sixth floor was a magnificent delicatessen that offered countless cheeses, sausages, and wines, and the seventh floor was home to fine restaurants. Truman Platz, an American military base, was just a short subway ride from their apartment and a place where they would shop or do laundry. Fine German restaurants offering traditional, heavy dishes were easy to find, as were Chinese restaurants and pizza joints, but Mexican restaurants were rare for some reason. West Berliners loved Americans, largely, Ryan thought, because of the Berlin airlift after World War II, when the Soviet Union threatened to choke off the western part of the city. He and Lexi could ride any bus, underground (U-Bahn), or surface rail (S-Bahn) anywhere in West Berlin just by flashing their military identification cards, a perk that made his many trips to Tegel airport virtually free. They also liked to spend a day in East Berlin on occasion. Being a retired navy officer, he could take Lexi on a military bus to East Berlin, and the two would merely show their identification cards at checkpoints. They would change deutschmarks to reichsmarks at the base before departure at a rate of seven reichsmarks for a deutschmark, while civilian tourists generally got only one for one at the checkpoints, so that was a nice perk as well.

East Berlin, however, was filled with a lot of Soviet-style architecture, in contrast to West Berlin, which reminded Ryan of Las Vegas—all lights and vibrancy. The boxy car, the *Trabant* or *Trabi*, was omnipresent in East Berlin. It had a two-cylinder, two-stroke engine, and the body was made largely of hardened plastic and recycled materials. It was a heavy polluter and really one of the worst cars ever made; it was often cited as a symbol of the failure of a centrally planned economy. Nonetheless, people in East Germany had to get on waiting lists of up to thirteen years to buy a *Trabi* or for any services for that matter. A man, one story went, ordered the car in 1964 and was told he could pick it up on December 1, 1972. The buyer asked, "Morning or afternoon?" The agent asked, "What does it matter after eight years?" The buyer said, "I have a plumber coming in the afternoon that day."

Ryan and Lexi tried to talk to East Berliners but found them to be very tight lipped; the Stasi, secret police, were everywhere and would report citizens for any suspicious activity.

One estimate had it that up to 2 million East Germans had worked for the Stasi at one time or another, and that was out of a population of 16 million. They once found a well-dressed gentleman who came up to them and *wanted* to talk to people who were obviously from West Berlin. He told them of a relative in the western part of the city he hadn't seen for years and complained about the six-month waiting time for a telephone and many more years for a Trabant. The only good things to buy were cameras, shoes, and porcelain, but it was difficult to find store clerks to wait on you; since there was no profit motive, clerks would stand around chatting rather than helping. Merchandising was poor, and many times what was on display in the window was not available for sale. Purchases got wrapped in newspaper and tied with string.

But East Berlin had many historic sites. There was the attractive Unter den Linden (under the linden trees) Avenue, which at one time was the main and most impressive boulevard in the city, the wonderful Pergamon museum with its many antiquities and considerable holdings of Islamic art, and various memorials to the Great Patriotic War. World War II resulted in the deaths of about 20 million Russians, while the United States had lost about 2 percent of that amount.

Back in their flat, Ryan asked Lexi whether she wanted to hear some airline jokes. She said yes, and he obliged. "This blonde was sitting in economy, extremely nervous about flying—especially after recent hijackings. She asked the man next to her, 'What are the chances of a bomb being on this airplane?' 'Mighty slim, maybe one in a hundred thousand,' he said. 'I don't like those odds. What are the chances of two bombs being on the plane?' she asked. 'Extremely unlikely, maybe one in a billion,' the guy said. 'Let me out of here!' she said. 'I have to go get a bomb.'"

"She had to be a blonde, huh?" Lexi retorted. "Just because I'm a blonde?"

"No. There's supposed to be something funny about dumb blondes. Not you, of course. How about this one? A blonde was sitting in first class, and a flight attendant asked to see her ticket. 'Ma'am, this ticket is for economy. Please move aft to your seat.' The blonde said, 'Everyone likes me and thinks I'm pretty, so they always put me in first class.' 'I'm sorry, but you'll have to move,' the attendant said. The blonde was adamant. 'I always fly this airline. They love me here, always put me in first class, and I'm not moving.' Exasperated, she told the first officer the situation. The copilot said, 'I'm married to a blonde; I know just what to do.' The copilot went to first class and asked the blonde, 'What's your destination, ma'am?' 'Prague,' she answered. The first officer said, 'Sorry, lady, first class is going to London.' 'In that case I'll move back.' the blonde said. 'I have to go to Prague.'"

"Another blonde went up to a ticket agent and said, 'I want to buy a round-trip ticket.' The agent asked, 'To where, ma'am?' She responded, 'To here, of course.'

"One more," Ryan told Lexi. "An airplane had an emergency shortly after takeoff from Los Angeles and dumped fuel over the ocean to get down to landing weight. The captain called the purser to the cockpit and asked if all the passengers were ready for landing. The purser said, 'Yes sir, except for the lawyers who're still handing out business cards.'"

"What a knee-slapper! Stop while you're ahead," Lexi said.

"Okay, no more jokes," Ryan said, "but one quick story. When I joined my first squadron, I had to serve as a navigator for a while. There were always three pilots in our crews, the junior one being the navigator. After some seasoning, the navigator would move to the right seat as copilot and eventually to the left seat as patrol plane commander, the PPC. New pilots would arrive in the squadron about once a month as older PPCs were transferred to new duty stations. The commander had the responsibility to train the other two pilots, so the navigator would often move to the cockpit and the copilot would navigate. A good plane commander would rotate all takeoffs and landings so the other two pilots could progress. These landings would take place from the left seat. PPCs would sometimes place a flashlight vertically on the cockpit floor, lens down, and challenge the pilot making the landing to make a 'squeaker' so that the flashlight wouldn't fall over. This was a difficult feat but could be done every now and then. When a pilot could accomplish that, it was a real confidence builder.

"I just thought of one more story that you may find amusing. During the final year in my first squadron, my copilot was a guy named Phil. He was a good guy—tall, athletic, and very religious. Well, our crew flew in and out of Viet Nam often while we were actually on deployment to Sangley Point in the Philippines. We would stay in Saigon for about two weeks and then rotate back to Sangley for a couple of weeks as we were replaced by another crew. We kept repeating this rotation for the six months deployment, although I left after five months to leave the navy for Contrails.

"Anyhow, Phil and I roomed together and got along well. We stayed at the Harding Hotel near the Rex where we ate our meals. Our hotel was sandbagged outside and manned by two guards behind the bags. One night, after we brushed our teeth with San Miguel beer—we certainly couldn't use the tap water—we read for awhile and fell asleep. In the middle of the night, we heard loud noises like gunfire and at the same time saw bright intermittent flashes. We both dove under our beds.

After things quieted down we turned on our flashlights which we kept by our beds along with our revolvers. After my first deployment, I always kept a snub-nosed detective special in an ankle holster or by my pillow. One of us said, 'What was that?' We looked around and saw that our air conditioner unit was smoking. Apparently it had shorted out during the night. It was a testament to the poor quality of the wiring and workmanship in the hotel. It also revealed how our nerves were constantly on edge walking around or just living in Saigon. It was not a funny episode at the time, but it was as Phil and I years later reminisced about our times in 'Nam."

CHAPTER THREE

All my bags are packed I'm ready to go
I'm standing here outside your door
I hate to wake you up to say goodbye ...
Already I'm so lonely I could die

—John Denver
Singer, songwriter, and pilot

O N ONE FINE MORNING, Ryan was sitting in the
cockpit in Frankfurt with Al Hartman, a captain
he'd known from an earlier pattern. Al had a Polish
girlfriend, a flight attendant named Petra, so he tried to bid trips
to Eastern Europe. The flight was direct to Warsaw and then to
Krakow. Direct flights meant passengers didn't have to change
aircraft, although some got off while others got on. Petra was
an attractive, well-built redhead. Polish stews always met the
cockpit crew in Frankfurt operations and flew exclusively to
Eastern Europe. Their salaries were low, but they made their
money with their per diems. German flight attendants flew
to the other locations in Europe. The pilots waited at the gate
for passenger loading and chitchatted before beginning the
prestart checklist. Al, definitely a man who liked women, had
a wife in America as well as this girlfriend in Europe.

One particular day they had a new Polish stew, Beata, and the purser brought her to the cockpit for a little orientation, much to the delight of Captain Hartman. She was quite a comely young woman with auburn hair and big brown eyes. "Do you know the difference, young lady, between sex and Caesar salad?" Al asked her.

Beata, not being very worldly, apparently didn't know about that particular salad and replied, "No sir, captain."

"Good, we'll have lunch after we land!"

She didn't really process that either, so Al pushed his luck. "Beata, would you go to bed with me for a hundred deutschmarks?"

"That is a lot of money, sir. Perhaps I would if we keep it quiet."

"Well, would you go to bed with me for five marks?" he asked.

"Of course not sir, what do you think I am?"

"We've already established that," Al answered. "We're just haggling over price." With that, she almost left the cockpit, but he added, "I'm just kidding you, Beata. Welcome to Contrails. To make it up to you, I'll let you steer the airplane on the ground." By that time they had gotten traffic control clearance. They finished the preliminary checklists, started the engines, and began taxiing.

"Just lean over my shoulder and turn this steering wheel, which we call the yoke," Al told Beata." It's just like a car." So the poor girl moved the yoke left and right, but she had to leave her feet and put her body all over his shoulders, neck, and back. In the meantime, unbeknownst to Beata, Al was manually controlling the nose-wheel steering on the lower left-hand console. He was all smiles, and the poor young lady didn't really understand. Finally, he said, "Well done. More lessons later. You'd better go back and strap in."

"What do you think Ryan—pretty sexy, huh?" Al asked Ryan.

"You need help, Al," was the best Ryan could add.

During the flight to Warsaw, Ryan said, "Al, I don't mean to pry, but I've flown with you before, and Petra is often in your monthly pattern. So you always bid Eastern European trips. You seem smitten with Petra and apparently fly with her as much as possible, but you have a wife in California. How does this all turn out down the road, if I may ask?"

"Well, life is short," Al said. "We have to live it as it comes, and fate or karma will dictate the future. What's an affair? What's infidelity? Is there a distinction without a difference? You'll find my situation isn't unique. In our profession, we fly to exotic places with beautiful women. During layovers, it's more or less natural for the entire flight crew to meet for dinner. Friendships and, yes, relationships are formed. It's only natural. It plays out as it will."

Indeed, Ryan knew several people from his flight training, his original squadron, or from his Contrails training classes who had had affairs that sometimes led to broken marriages. This occurred not only in Contrails but in other airlines as well. Ken, one of Ryan's friends from his first navy squadron, didn't show up one time in the hotel lobby in Antigua for a crew pickup at 7:00 a.m. After waiting a few minutes, the captain asked the hotel clerk for the key to his room. Ken was asleep with a female flight attendant and several empty champagne bottles. He was drunk, and the flight got delayed for a day until another flight engineer, where newly hired pilots began their cockpit careers, was flown in. Ken had gotten fired, and the union had no grounds to save his career.

Ryan visited Ken at his home a couple of months later. He told him he was sorry about what had happened, and Ken admitted he'd been stupid. Ryan asked what his plans were, and Ken said he might try to work for another airline, but somehow the incident would be in the network somewhere, and he would have to lie on any job application. He shrugged and said he might work for the Federal Aviation Administration. Ryan crossed his arms and said, "There's an old joke that goes, 'Nobody knew I drank until I showed up sober one morning.' For you, it might be that people thought you didn't drink until you showed up drunk one morning. Do you drink a lot, Ken?"

"Yes, probably too much. I do have hangovers."

"Well, my uncle had that problem. One time he drank 'Canada Dry'—literally. But if you don't want to have hangovers, just stay drunk. Seriously, Ken, you can beat this. If drinking affects your life, get help. Try Alcoholics Anonymous or see a doctor. You're young. Think it through. Call me anytime."

This incident reminded Ryan of the old saying that social drinking in the navy was the same as acute alcoholism in the air force. The navy's rule was no drinking within eight hours of a flight and no smoking within fifty feet of an aircraft. Some pilots jokingly thought this should be no drinking within fifty feet of the aircraft and no smoking within eight hours of a flight. Some crewmembers smoked while airborne, but in patrol planes, most pilots didn't know what went on in the back of the aircraft. Indeed, naval aviators played hard and drank hard. Back in the 1960s and '70s, there were happy hours a couple of times a week. A squadron's commanding officer could call one on any day at about 4:00 p.m., and everyone would head to the officers' club. Ryan recalled one day when the announcement came that two of his unit's commanders had been selected for captain, so all the officers headed to the club early to celebrate. This was fine, except that Ryan played on an intramural basketball team and had a game scheduled for 5:15. He gulped down several drinks and headed to the gym around 4:30 or so. He normally had a pretty good jump shot and sank about 50 percent of his shots from fifteen to twenty feet. This particular day, every time he went up to shoot he saw two baskets, so his percentage went down to about twenty-five percent, and his tongue felt like cotton the whole game.

Ryan remembered that during the Vietnam War, aircraft carriers would come off Yankee Station near North Vietnam and pull into Naval Station Subic Bay in the Philippines for a little rest and relaxation. The flight crews had sometimes flown two or three flights a day for weeks on end when on station. When their ship went into port, the officers' club at Cubi Point Naval Air Station, adjacent to Subic Bay went wild as the cockpit crewmembers unleashed all their pent-up tension and celebrated the fact they were still alive.

Ryan knew that commercial airline flying was indeed rough on marriages. At one time in airline history, Pan Am used to fly around-the-world trips leaving east and west from New York, and the crew would stay together for about two weeks. With layovers in exotic places, relationships were formed, and romances blossomed. This was the golden age of airline flying. The Pan Am wives' group eventually convinced management that after a few days, crews had to be broken up at certain places even if it added a day to the whole pattern.

During the flight to Warsaw, one flight attendant entered the cockpit and asked the crewmembers if they needed coffee or a soda. When she turned to Ryan, their eyes met and held for a second or two. He was stunned by her beauty. She had black hair, green eyes, and a porcelain complexion with a slight Mediterranean hue. She was maybe five foot five and well proportioned. She wore little makeup—maybe a light blush. She kept her hair short, with a slight wave, and at collar level.

She had full lips and a very slight upturn in her nose. There was a flash of chemistry, like two atoms combining into a molecule. He saw innocence and an easy grace in her eyes. He asked for a black coffee and said, "We haven't met. I'm Ryan, Ryan Lasseter." "I'm Katarina Mueller. Nice to meet you. I'll get your coffee. Perhaps we'll talk at dinner."

Ryan sensed something else in those eyes. He had seen it in Miami, on his first tour with Contrails years earlier, when he had been a flight engineer. A Norwegian stewardess had come to the cockpit asking if anybody wanted drinks. She had beautiful Nordic features—blonde hair and azure-blue eyes. She hesitated after taking their orders. Ryan saw a glisten in her eyes and perhaps sadness. He quietly said, "I see from your name tag your name's Britta. Listen, please tell me if you're homesick. I know you're flying with American girls mainly. If you're lonely, you can confide in me—honestly. I can tell—I can empathize. Listen, Britta, I sense you feel, well, maybe out of place. We have few European stewardesses here. If you want, my wife is picking me up at the airport. Would you like to go out to dinner with us? We can talk. I have Scandinavian heritage—let us help you. We'll drive you to your place after we eat and visit."

The three went out to dinner, and Britta opened up. She admitted she missed her family and Norway tremendously. Ryan said, "Perhaps you and Claire can shop and do things together." Britta seemed excited by this. They later did things together, and Claire was hopeful that the intervention helped.

Recalling this, Ryan saw in Katarina's eyes much more than goodness, beauty, intellect, and awareness—he saw melancholy. Then he had an epiphany—Katarina was the stew he'd seen on his first trip to the Soviet Union.

Lexi was not with Ryan on that trip—she had to be with

31

her sick sister in Virginia, which was not uncommon. He checked into his room in Warsaw and had a couple of hours to kill before dinner. That's when another realization hit him; Katarina was the mystery woman he had seen at that restaurant in Frankfurt! He put on a rain jacket and set out for a very depressing walk. He saw small grocery stores with chickens hung by hooks in the open air. The vegetables looked rotten. Strolling further among the large, gray buildings, he came upon a museum of science and technology. He toured that, found it interesting, and headed back to the hotel.

The crew met in the lobby and walked a few blocks to the Unicorn restaurant in the area which was part of the Jewish ghetto in World War II. Ryan "happened" to sit by Katarina. They engaged in small talk more or less apart from the others, and he said, "You have no accent. You sound like an American. Don't you live here in Poland ... Katarina?"

"Well, I am an American," she said. "In fact, my father is the chief legal counsel for Contrails. I received an MBA from Wharton last year, and my dad secured a position for me with our company. He wanted me first to learn the workings of the company from the bottom up. I worked as a flight attendant in New York for a few months. I took some time off, traveled with friends, and then he arranged for me to be based in Berlin to learn the European operations. As you know, it's generally Polish flight attendants who fly to Eastern Bloc countries, but he worked it out so I could fly anywhere in Europe. I like it, although I sometimes feel like a fish out of water being the only American flight attendant here. I'd been in college for six years and am glad to see more of the world and learn how the operating side of the company works before I start in on the financial end. By the way, you can call me Kate." She relayed all this without a hint of haughtiness or braggadocio.

"Where did you go to high school, and where does your family live?" Ryan asked.

"We live in Atherton, California. I went to Palo Alto High. My dad commutes to the San Francisco Airport, where Contrails headquarters are."

"Atherton's an expensive area. I thought maybe you went to prep school."

"No, Atherton was great—close to San Francisco. I played varsity tennis and was in student government in high school. I also performed in student plays. I guess I had a lot of energy."

"What an interesting story. Wharton. Wow, wonderful school for business. Where did you get your undergraduate degree? Stanford, I'm betting?"

"Yes, and I loved it."

"Why didn't you get an MBA at Stanford, which has a stellar graduate business program?"

"I loved Stanford, but I suppose I thought going to Wharton might broaden my curriculum vitae."

"Well, that's amazing. I also went to Stanford—aeronautical engineering. Probably about twenty years or more before you, I'd imagine. When I first entered college, the first five people I met had all gone to prestigious prep schools. Well, we have a lot to talk about. Stanford's noted for its academic excellence, and it's such a beautiful campus. Its climate is wonderful, and, what amazes me is that Stanford has about one-third the student population of the big PAC-10 schools, but it's won more NCAA championships than any other school except UCLA. Their great athletes are truly student athletes."

"I thought about playing varsity tennis there," Kate said, "but I just couldn't fit it in. I had a dual major—economics and political science. I played a lot as a junior. The chance I'd make that team was slim at any rate. They win a lot of championships."

"Actually, we have something else in common. I have an MBA too. When I first joined Contrails, I was based in Miami and was a flight engineer on Boeing 727s. I was so bored in that position and had about thirteen days a month off, so I decided to get my MBA at night at the University of Miami. I won the position of vice chairman of our union so I could get preferential bidding. So I flew mainly on weekends and went to school at night. I really didn't do any union work, and I'm pro-management anyhow. Got the degree in three years. Miami is no Wharton, but it was the only game in town. On layovers, when the rest of the crew was partying, I was busy typing papers. I'm sure I could've gotten into one of the top business schools since I did well as an undergraduate and scored very high on the Graduate Management Admissions Test. But I had a career going, and with a family I certainly couldn't afford to go to graduate school full-time for two years and change directions for my future. Also, I thought the furlough would last for only a couple of years. But really, the allure of being an airline pilot was too much to pass up. You get great pay and a lot of time off, and you travel to exotic places doing something you love. The retirement's wonderful, and there are many perks. Econ and poly sci as majors. Any thought of going into politics some day?"

"What, and become a member of the House of Representatives some day? With a two-year term, those pols spend the first year learning the job and the second year running for reelection. You would have to serve several terms to make any sort of an impact. That doesn't seem like self-actualization to me. Party politics seems to make Congress dysfunctional in many ways. There are some fine congressmen, though. Senator Henry 'Scoop' Jackson of Washington is an example of someone who can cut across party lines. Mark Twain said, 'No man's life, liberty, or happiness is safe when the legislature is in session.' And President Lincoln said, 'Nearly all men can stand adversity, but if you want to test a man's character, give him power.'"

"A little cynical, but okay. What did you specialize in at Wharton?"

"Finance. I'll be working the whole gamut in that field. Fine-tuning capitalization, lease-buy decisions, mergers and acquisitions, vertical-integration opportunities, investment of surplus capital, and so forth."

"That's fascinating, and a lot of things to take on. More to talk about."

"Of course, I wouldn't be involved in all those issues at once. Those are just some of the things I'll get into."

On some level there was a mind-meld going on. After they got to their hotel, Katarina and Ryan had a couple of schnapps in the bar, peppermint for her and peach for him. They talked about college, sports, hangout places such as Rossotti's, L'Ommie's, and Delmonico's, and professors they may have had in common. Ryan had studied engineering but had to take a sprinkling of liberal arts courses.

After a time they bade each other good night. Ryan couldn't get her out of his mind and had a restless sleep. There was a cognitive dissonance going on here—how could something that seemed so incredibly right be undeniably wrong?

He flew with Katarina again a few times while Lexi was in Virginia. He and Katarina would often have dinner or drinks and just talk. During their second dinner together, she said, "Ryan, you paid for my meal the first time, so from now on it's dutch treat. It was chivalry at first, but after that it would be dating—we're not doing that. We're just enjoying each other's company. I don't want to be a kept woman. Besides, you know I'm not poor."

Their relationship was getting closer. He knew the day

would come, and soon, when Lexi and Katarina would be on the same flight with him. He actually looked forward to it but pondered how he would deal with it.

One night at dinner in Munich, Katarina and Ryan dined by themselves at a traditional German restaurant in Marienplatz with its famous glockenspiel. They enjoyed sauerbraten, spaetzel, and strudel. He asked her, "Kate, do you think these dinners and talks, well, you might say liaisons, actually constitute dating?"

"You have my phone number in Berlin, where I live," she answered. "You've never called to ask me out. These aren't dates—we just enjoy being with each other on these layovers. Even though we stay away from the other crewmembers for these encounters, and the flight attendants do talk, believe me, they aren't trysts. By the way, a couple of your comments imply I'm perfect—I'm far from that. What do you think of our meetings?"

"Well, as you know I'm happily married, so I can't even entertain the thought of dating, but I look forward to being with you and cherish these times. I consider myself an honorable man, yet I am a man. You say you're not perfect, but who is?"

"Please, let's change the subject. Why don't you tell me more about your flying? I didn't take any engineering courses at Stanford, but I remember from high school physics something about Bernoulli. How do these machines fly?"

"You're right about Bernoulli being involved. His theorem was that when the velocity of a fluid increases, its pressure drops, so picture the cross section of a wing. The top has a significant curve, called camber, and the bottom is rather flat. Air travels faster over the top of the wing than it does at the bottom, so you have lower pressure on the top of the wing and higher pressure on the bottom—hence lift. For a body to be in equilibrium, all forces and moments must be equal, so the weight of the airplane is offset by the lift. That's the quick and dirty. You have to have equilibrium on the vertical, lateral, and longitudinal axes for stability. That translates to yaw, pitch, and roll. But that's for another day.

"Anyhow, for background, I flew multiengine patrol planes with a basic mission of antisubmarine warfare. We could carry rockets, mines, and torpedoes— even nuclear ones. We did a lot of reconnaissance work. Mainly, it was long hours of boredom interrupted by moments of stark terror. In my first tour, I made three six-month deployments to the western Pacific, two in Japan and one in the Philippines. We would send detachments to Vietnam for a couple of weeks or so and kept rotating crews. We had twelve airplanes in the squadron and usually kept three or four in Vietnam at a time.

"In 'Nam we did coastal surveillance twenty-four hours a day in coordination with a similar squadron, looking for junks or sampans infiltrating arms. We also did what we called 'rigging' of merchant ships in the daytime to see what countries were sending ships into those waters. We'd fly at a hundred feet over the water photographing both sides and the stern of the ship to check on its registration and cargo.

"Flying there was especially dangerous at night when, for example, we'd detect a target three miles off the coast and have to identify it. Our radar altimeter would be set to one hundred feet to warn us if we went below that height above the water. A light would come on below that point. Usually there was no horizon. The radar operator would guide us into the target, and we would illuminate it with a one-million candlepower searchlight. Sometimes we would first drop parachute flares from a higher altitude to light up the sky and then go low. That was eerie. Occasionally, we would find a suspicious boat near the coast and call in a Coast Guard cutter for an inspection. We lost several planes during this operation—from our squadron and sister squadrons. I recall that one flew into the water and a few were shot down.

"When we didn't fly, we lived in a hotel in Saigon, which was an interesting city with a definite French influence left over from their occupation in the 1950s. There were good French and Vietnamese restaurants in the city, and it was always exciting to walk down Tu Do Street and watch the women in their flowing *au dai* dresses, hearing the girls saying, "Hey GI, you numba one," and to see all the black-market vendors selling things that had obviously come from a US military post exchange. Saigon had unique aromas, which were generally not pleasant. People hawked grilled meat, undoubtedly dog, on many corners. All those omnipresent small mopeds and mini-taxis put out choking fumes, and occasionally you'd catch a whiff of cordite.

"The officers generally ate at the Rex hotel, which had been commandeered by the United States military. We'd have drinks before dinner in the open-air, canopied top floor of the hotel. A Vietnamese band and various singers would entertain us. It was well known that the vocalists didn't speak English but had memorized most of the current American hit songs. Often, during drinks, we could see aircraft dropping bombs several miles away. I knew my memories would last a long time.

"One interesting story involved the time when six of us officers stayed in the same room at the Majestic Hotel by the Mekong River in downtown Saigon. As we went to sleep, we'd all put our wallets and watches by our nightstands. One morning we woke up to find all our valuables missing. Someone had come in during the wee hours and stolen them. The one exception was a friend of mine who kept everything, including a thirty-two caliber pistol, inside his pillowcase. I teased him later that if he had awakened and had shot the thief, the whole outcome of the war might have changed if the bad guy had been Viet Cong. We reported the theft, of course, but the police just laughed at us in their own way and wished us good luck.

"Another time, this same friend and I were piloting our plane on an airway going west over Korea very near the demilitarized zone (DMZ). Over the radio, we received an instruction in perfect English with our call sign to 'Turn right to 350 degrees for traffic separation.' We looked at each other, understanding immediately that the turn would take us into North Korea. If we had made that turn, there was a good chance we would have been shot down by a missile. So I responded, 'Station calling, you are garbled. Say again.' They repeated the instruction. I said again, 'You are garbled, proceeding on track.' That could have been an international incident."

"I'm curious about these vertical fins I see at the wingtips of some airplanes," she asked. "What are they for?"

"They're called winglets, and they prevent energy loss from wing tip vortices. Or rather, they minimize the vortices. On a regular wing, the high-pressure air under the wing tends to bend over the tip to replace or disrupt the low-pressure on top, and that reduces lift somewhat. The winglets mitigate that to some degree. The vortices propel downward and aft of the aircraft. In fact, those vortices are very powerful, like a cyclone, and could upset a small aircraft. The larger the airplane, the more lift is needed, and hence the vortices are stronger on heavy aircraft. Large aircraft must use the word "heavy" in their call sign, such as 'Contrails 128 heavy at flight level 330.'"

"Fascinating. How did you end up at Contrails?"

"Well, I got out of the navy after my first tour, joined the company for a few years—that's when I was in Miami—then Contrails furloughed about six hundred pilots after they got thirty-some Boeing 747s that replaced the old 707s on a two-for-one basis or more. I returned to the navy, was in two more squadrons, was in charge of one of them, went to graduate school for an MS in aeronautical engineering, served six years at the Pentagon, and went to the National Defense University for about a year. When I retired, I returned to Contrails, which had kept my seniority number—they had to do that by law since I had various military commitments because of schools and promotions.

"As you know, in business school we learned micro and macroeconomics, accounting, finance, analytical analysis, and marketing. Marketing involves all the activities that it takes to get a product from the producer to the consumer. That includes advertising, pricing, channels of distribution, and merchandising. But I found out that, at least in my business school, leadership wasn't really taught. I learned that in the navy. First in ROTC and then as a plane commander with eleven crewmembers. We had to work as a team. Later I had my own squadron where good leadership was a must. You must always take care of your people. You have to set an example in appearance and behavior. You learn to praise in public and reprimand in private. Mainly, leadership comes from helping people fulfill their needs, such as social, esteem, and self-actualization. Without good leadership you have no morale, and without morale things become hopeless. That reminds me of the movie *Caine Mutiny*.

"Now, there's something I should tell you on a totally different subject. When I was at the Pentagon, I got divorced. Claire and I were happily married for many years, but we grew apart. She went to UC Berkeley, and we dated throughout college. Later in my career, she began a career she loved, our kids were in college, and it ended up as well as those things can. Lexi became my second wife when I joined Contrails the second time."

"Divorce doesn't sound pleasant, but it happens; no shame in that. Everlasting love is almost impossible to find."

"Anyhow, before I got out of the navy the first time, I'd applied for and received job offers with seven airlines. I suppose I got so many offers because I had an engineering degree and many hours of multiengine flying. Plus, I assume I did well during my interviews. But I had friends who just wanted to get out of the navy and then look for a job with an airline. I always counseled them to remember the first law of wing walking: 'Never let go of what you have until you have hold of something else.' I also told them that until they obtained a job with an airline, they were losing seniority.

"Another story that you might find interesting is this. Just before I left the navy the first time, I was deployed in the Philippines, and Claire was with me. She was quite pregnant at the time, but we still did some adventurous things, like white-water rafting, on that deployment. I left the squadron before it was due to return to the United States. We flew from Manila to San Francisco with Pan Am. I was out-processed at Treasure Island Naval Station in San Francisco. I completed my training with Contrails at their facilities in San Francisco. Claire was nine months pregnant on our flight to Miami to begin route flying with the company. We'd have to find a place to live, find a doctor and a hospital, and I'd begin flying. We knew no one in Miami. But on that flight I had crab cocktail and also ate my son's serving of the same appetizer. Before we landed, my neck started to swell, and my pulse was racing. We landed otherwise uneventfully, rented a car, found a motel, and Claire called a doctor. It turned out I'd gone into anaphylactic shock. The doctor gave me adrenaline and cortisone, but I could hardly stand. He told me never to have crab again.

"Actually, I'd experienced a similar problem while I was in the navy. We flew to Kodiak, Alaska often, and I'd bring a lot of frozen king crabs back to Whidbey Island. We kept them in the bomb bay to stay cold. We loved that food. Well one night, after eating crab, I broke out in hives. We went to a doctor who was unsure of the diagnosis—I wasn't in shock. I'd chopped wood that day, and I told him I may have been bitten by a spider, and also that I had eaten crab. He told me to try crab again sometime to see what happened. It turned out to be bad advice, obviously.

"I was lucky during my career—I lost many friends from flight training both in Vietnam and in other accidents outside the war zone. I knew a couple of pilots who were prisoners of war for a long time. But I've talked a long time, Kate, about war stories. I'm sure you're bored. Tell me more about yourself."

"I will, Ryan, but I love these stories. We'll get back to them. For now let me just tell you my family's wealthy. I played a lot of tennis as a junior and was, in fact, ranked nationally in the sixteen-and-under age bracket. I was also in Mensa. You know what that is?"

"Yes, of course; it's a group for people in the top two percent of the population in IQ. Very impressive. "

"I'm bragging, but you asked. I need to tell you about an important part of my life. When I was in elementary and secondary schools, I had a serious problem with stuttering, and it took a lot of therapy and work to overcome it. I'm not sure it's completely cured. I had a real problem with some consonants, but the speech therapist did wonders. One thing I found helpful was singing—I didn't stutter as much when I sang. In fact, I played Maria in a high school performance of *West Side Story*. I could really belt out 'Tonight.' I had a crush on Jared, who played Tony in the performance. We were pretty close, but I found out as I entered my teens and developed, other guys would try to get close to me. It turned out that 'Na … *No*' was more emphatic than just 'No.'"

"I went through the stuttering until about my junior year in high school. It hurt my self-esteem but not my sense of self-worth. I could sing well, but not well enough for serious competition. The singing really did help me. When you sing a song, there's a chain of words—there's no real thinking to follow one word with another as long as you've memorized the words. Compare that to natural conversation, where you're constantly searching for the next word. I believe I'm pretty much c-cured. There you go. Still working on it."

"That problem must have been incredibly hard on you. I can sense the frustration you must have felt when you couldn't keep your thoughts flowing. It's amazing you overcame it. But now, Kate, you're absolutely normal in that area. Most people stumble over words or pronunciations. No more worries, mate."

"Thank you. I'm not comfortable talking a lot about myself, and I enjoy your war stories. So tell me more."

"Well, *you* tell an interesting story. You seem to have no problem with words now. I hate to bore you, so stop me when you've had enough. I'm quite a talker. But back to the stories. One fellow pilot, a friend of mine, happened to be Japanese-American. During World War II, when he was about four, his family was put into an internment camp, which was policy even for United States citizens of that ethnicity at that time. In 1972, his plane was shot down over North Vietnam, and for the second time in his life he was interned. Quite a story. He should write a book.

"Here's one more. The last admiral I worked for was a navy pilot who was shot down over 'Nam in 1965. He came home in '73—eight years as a prisoner. He came back, got a PhD in electrical engineering, and later made admiral. His wonderful wife didn't leave him, as some did, and wisely invested his income all those years. He was one of the first pilots shot down over there. He told Claire and me over dinner at his house that he kept his sanity during those years as a prisoner by building his dream home in his mind, brick by brick. About fifteen years after his return, he did build that very home in Virginia. He also kept his mind by composing music in his head and by teaching advanced math to fellow prisoners when they could mingle near the end of their captivity. He was a fine officer with great fortitude. During the early years of his confinement, he was tortured brutally. There but for the grace of God …

"I was also fortunate in that my family came with me on my deployments. We were usually overseas for about six months and kept a house in the local community in Japan and the Philippines. When we weren't in 'Nam, we'd fly patrols in the Sea of Japan or the Yellow Sea or in the South China Sea, always looking for merchant ships or gaining intelligence in other ways. We'd often fly very close to Russia, and in fact, one of our squadron airplanes was hit by a missile in the Straits of Tsushima, by the Kuril Islands, a disputed area between Russia and Japan, and had some damage on a wing. The plane made it back safely, but it could have been disastrous.

"All this was in the late 1960s, when the Cold War was going strong and so was the war in Vietnam. The war was a farce in many ways. The military was hamstrung by Congress and the president when it came to choosing targets. Drugs were rampant, and beer was regularly flown to forward operating bases. What a way to fight a war.

"The biggest danger we faced while flying in South Vietnam was a shoot-down in the Mekong delta or a ditching off the coast. With eleven crewmembers, those of us who would have survived such a downing would have little chance if we'd been captured by the Viet Cong. If found by a small patrol of VC, we might have had a fighting chance with our revolvers, although we probably would've been up against automatic weapons. But if found by a group of platoon size or larger, we would've been tortured severely and spent the rest of our probably brief lives in bamboo cages. If we happened to be discovered by friendly South Vietnamese, our chances were much better.

"We'd carry a fair amount of dong, the currency of the South, in our survival vests. Plus we had a 'blood chit,' a piece of cloth with wording that guaranteed a large amount of money if we were returned to American forces. If we had to survive on our own for a few days, our chances were iffy. We had maps of the South, flares, candy, a compass, water purification tablets, waterproof matches, and individualized items such as fishing hooks and line, more candy, a penlight, and so forth. Whatever we carried had to fit in our flight suit or vests. Otherwise, we carried no wallets, no identification cards, no wedding rings—only dog tags.

"We had a favorite routine when flying the Sea of Japan in the winter. We'd get up at five in the morning for a six o'clock brief and a seven o'clock takeoff. We had to wear rubberized anti-exposure suits for the ten-hour flight. They were heavy, bulky, hot, and uncomfortable, but if we ever had to ditch, they would keep us alive for about fifteen minutes longer than otherwise. Hardly worth the effort.

"After landing at about five in the afternoon, we would debrief, shower, change, and head for the officers' club annex for a *hotsi* bath. We would strip naked, get into a very hot pool of water, wash again, wrap a towel around us, lie on a table, and then get a massage from a Japanese woman. It was very relaxing and got all the kinks out. The women, being light in weight, would walk on our backs. After dressing, we would get a taxi to the Anchor Grill restaurant in Iwakuni for a delicious Kobe beef dinner with Kirin beer. We slept very well those evenings.

"One rather funny story involved me riding a bike from our base to our home in Iwakuni after a late flight. About midnight, as I was riding, a saw a couple under a street light.

The American man happened to be my commanding officer, and the woman was Japanese. We locked eyes, the man looked down, but I just rode home. I kept this story to myself for years. There'd be no gain in telling it to my friends, except for a few chuckles, but there'd be a lot of pain if the story got out to the squadron. I'm rambling, talking way too much about myself and flying. Aren't you tired of this?"

"No, I find it most interesting. Go on."

"At first, most of us believed in our presence in 'Nam. We believed in the 'domino theory.' We'd been sent there to stop the spread of communism. As the war dragged on, I began to realize the fighting in the country was basically a civil war. We had no exit policy, and the public was not behind our effort. The year 1968 was a pivotal year, riots at the Democratic convention in Chicago, the assassinations of Martin Luther King and Bobby Kennedy, the capture of the *Pueblo*, and the William Calley massacre of civilians in 'Nam. The whole war was a turning point in American society. People began to question authority. The sexual revolution started. 'Make love, not war.' You were young but saw the sexual revolution growing up—I didn't when I was in high school and college. That put a new focus on things in our society. Anyhow, it's getting late. The next time, I need to hear much more of your story, Kate. This was way too much about me. Shall we head on back?"

"Yes, but my life was uneventful compared to yours. I mean I had friends, did well in sports, traveled with my family, enjoyed learning, and strove to excel. I was in a beauty contest, which I say with modesty. More about that at another time. I loved college immensely, in all respects. We'll talk more about all this later. Let's get some sleep. It's an early wakeup."

Ryan wrestled through another sleepless night, wondering where things were headed. The force of this woman's persona had moved him so much that he knew his life would never be the same. His values and standards had been rearranged. He had to be a hopeless romantic. He was always reaching. He would get misty hiking in Yosemite Valley, listening to a recording of Edith Piaf singing *La Vie en Rose*, or seeing a picture of Grace Kelly. Perfection just moved him that much. In his mind, he truly wanted it all. As the son of a steelworker, he wanted to be the best, even to have things beyond what were obtainable. He just wasn't satisfied with "good enough."

CHAPTER FOUR

I wish that I could fly
Into the sky
So very high
Just like a dragonfly

—Lenny Kravitz

RYAN WAS FLYING WITH Tim House, a congenial guy with whom he had flown previously on a one-day pattern to Hamburg. They had departed from Geneva for Istanbul and were flying at thirty-three thousand feet and at Mach .82. Taking off to the east from Geneva was a flying experience in itself. Pilots had to make certain altitude checkpoints at mile markers or else go into holding patterns to gain altitude, all to make sure they didn't run into Mont Blanc, the highest mountain in the Alps.

They started with the small talk. "Hey Ryan, if our wings come off here, how long would it take to die by falling this far?"

"The rest of your life," Ryan answered. "But remember, Tim, it's not the fall but the sudden stop. But it would take … oh about forty-five seconds in a vacuum, but about a minute because of the drag."

"How'd you come up with that?"

"I just know the laws of physics, and that's an easy question. But many folks would probably die of heart attacks before they hit the ground. When you fall like that, you reach terminal velocity, where gravity is offset by drag, and that's about a hundred miles per hour depending on your drag coefficient—whether you fall vertically or horizontally with respect to the ground. Do you know that as a passenger it's safer to fly in the back of the plane?"

Craig Fleming, the flight engineer, chimed in: "I don't think that's been proven."

Ryan said, "Well, have you ever heard of an aircraft backing into a mountain?"

"Okay smarty," Tim said. "You know when you talk to the passengers before landing, you have to give them the arrival airport's weather, including temperature in Celsius and Fahrenheit, but the airport terminal radios you the temp in Celsius only. How do you convert to Fahrenheit?"

"I simply use a conversion chart," Ryan answered.

"There's an easier way to do it," Tim said. "Just double the Celsius, subtract ten percent of that, and add thirty-two. It's easy and accurate"

Ryan recalled his old physics and realized Tim was right. Twenty degrees Celsius was in fact sixty-eight Fahrenheit. That made his life a little easier for his talks to the passengers.

"Al, I got a graduate degree in aeronautical engineering while in the navy. I was in the program when lasers were just coming into use, along with carbon-fiber materials and hand-held scientific calculators. We used to talk about the theory of circular runways. Have you ever heard of that?"

"No."

"Well, think about it. With a circular runway, you'd never run out of runway or land short or long. You could always land into the wind. Of course, you'd have to have a banked runway and a radius of five miles or so. Various spokes or radii would serve as taxiways, and the terminal would be the center of the circle with plenty of underground parking. The downside is that you'd need at least eighty square miles for the airport, which is pretty unrealistic these days."

"Interesting idea. What else do you have in mind?"

"Pilots talk about trading airspeed for altitude and vice versa, but engineers think in terms of trading potential energy for kinetic energy or the other way around. As cities get more congested, what about off-shore airports, like giant aircraft carriers? You could also move those into the wind. The problem here's that you'd need a lot of unique ferries or bridges to handle the automobile traffic. Tuck this away for the twenty-second century. Do you ever wonder how many ways an airplane can go down?"

"Well, human error, terrorism, and mechanical failure basically."

"Of course there are acts of God such as bird strikes, extreme turbulence, wind shear, microbursts, or perhaps flying over an erupting volcano before any warnings have been issued. As you know, lightning itself will not knock you out of the sky."

Their small talk was interrupted by frequency changes and so forth, but Ryan continued. "Do you recall the old days when we would lay over in exotic places like Trinidad or Antigua, and the stews would take all those little alcohol bottles off the airplane, and we'd have crew parties by the hotel pool?"

"Right. And now you never greet an old friend at an airport by saying 'Hi, Jack.'"

"Yep, days long gone. Now they're cutting our pay and messing with our medical insurance, not to mention our huge unfunded pension liability. But it's still a great job. What I like best is that you never take work home with you after your office job is done."

"Okay, what does the Australian airline name Qantas mean?" Tim asked.

"It means Queensland and Northern Territories Aerial Services. It goes back to the 1920s."

"All right, final question, for the jackpot. What does the BMW car logo depict?"

"Can't get me, Al. The blue and white roundel, so the story goes, depicts a white propeller with a blue-sky background. Bavarian Motor Works built aircraft engines long ago. Back to temperature scales, we have the Kelvin scale where zero is absolute zero—no atomic action of any kind. We have Celsius, which some still call centigrade, and we have Fahrenheit. It drives engineers nuts, although we deal with it. We need standardization."

"No more trivial pursuit with you, Ryan. You're too good."

"Have you ever been to Istanbul?" Tim asked Ryan.

"No, but I look forward to it. Tell me about it."

"Real interesting history. It sits on a hill overlooking the Bosporus, one of the world's most important waterways. It's an Islamic culture, but Turkey is part of NATO. The shopping and food are wonderful. I'll give you a tour. By the way, you know how they treat first-time drunk drivers in Istanbul? They strip them, drive them into the desert about twenty-five miles out of town, and leave them there with no clothes, no money, no water."

"Wow, what do they do for the second offense?"

"You don't wanna know."

They got rooms in a very nice InterContinental that overlooked the city and the Bosporus. The three cockpit members met in the lobby and started walking. Tim said, "You must buy custom-made shoes here. They measure you, and they'll be ready in a week or so or on your next trip. And the

51

price is right." They found the place, and Ryan got measured for half boots, zip style, for flying. They were soft leather, and he looked forward to picking them up. A taxi took them to the main bazaar, and Ryan learned that Istanbul taxi drivers were the worst. They met face-to-face with another taxi going the other way on a dark, narrow street. The drivers got out and got into a fist fight for the right-of-way. Their driver had won, but it shook them up a bit. They explored the bazaar, where they had knockoff Rolex watches for $25 and Louis Vuitton luggage for almost nothing. The vendors pursued them, tugged at their sleeves, just relentless. They had to physically push them away.

They had kabobs, sausages, vegetables, rice, beer, and something like baklava for dessert at a nice restaurant they found. They took an uneventful trip by cab back to the hotel. About 11:00 p.m., Ryan got a call from the captain. "Ryan, I'm terribly sick. I feel like I'm going to die. Call a doctor now."

Ryan called the front desk for a doctor pronto and went to Tim's room. Tim opened the door looking terrible. Ryan sat while Tim made several trips to the bathroom to purge.

"Tim, I'm guessing food poisoning here. The engineer and I are okay, but it seems you ate or drank something bad. Did you drink the water at that restaurant? Water here is a no-no." When Tim acknowledged he had, Ryan felt fairly certain it was food poisoning. The doctor who showed up about forty-five minutes later confirmed that suspicion and told the captain he wouldn't be flying the next day.

Ryan called Contrails operations and was told to enjoy the next day off because their flight would be canceled; they'd be flying an empty aircraft home the following day.

Ryan took a tour of the city the next morning after a bite to eat at the hotel. He walked for a couple of hours and came across a Turkish military officers' club. Since Turkey was a member of NATO and he had his military retiree card, he thought he'd try lunch there. Although the maître d' spoke little English, Ryan enjoyed a good curry lunch. After lunch, he took a cab to the bazaar again and bought a few small gifts. Then he went to the Hagia Sofia mosque, which was then a museum, and then to the Sultan Ahmen Mosque, or Blue Mosque. He took off his shoes, entered, and saw the men kneeling, facing Mecca, and performing their prayers. He was amazed at the beauty of the structure.

Later, it was back to the hotel to check on Tim, who felt weak but better. Ryan called the flight engineer to ask if he wanted dinner, and Craig readily agreed. He was the epitome of a navy fighter jock—an Annapolis grad and totally squared away. Over the meal, Craig mentioned that while he had been too young to fly in 'Nam, he had gone to the navy "Top Gun" school, a program for the very best fighter pilots. He enjoyed that experience but said, "I got discouraged by the fact that as I got more senior I'd be flying no more, something like you. I loved flying, so here I am."

After dinner, Ryan did some reading and sat on the balcony with a mini-bar beer, just enjoying the sight of the vibrant city. He felt grateful he had seen so much of the world. Istanbul was a nice little vacation in an exotic spot, and he was on the company's clock the whole time. Istanbul was the only city he knew of that sat on two continents.

He thought of his humble beginnings and of his college days. He had to attend the summer quarter at Stanford in '62 to graduate. Having taken three units of NROTC classes for twelve quarters meant he had to take three more courses to graduate. He took French novels, scientific writing, and thermodynamics. The French class involved reading books by Zola, Stendhal, Balzac, Flaubert, and others. He had to write a paper on each book, but there was no final. Claire did much of this work for Ryan since she had already finished college and had a simple clerical job to bide time before they would marry. The course load was light, so the couple enjoyed the summer and planned their wedding.

Stanford in the '60s had a strict grading curve. Professors had to average course grades for those who passed in the following manner: 15 percent got As, 35 percent got Bs; 35 percent Cs, and 15 percent Ds. This naturally varied from course to course, but the faculty had to meet this average over time. It would seem to follow that the overall student body grade point average would be 2.5 on a 4.0 scale, but since some people failed courses, the overall average hovered around 2.3. After all the protests during the Vietnam War, there was tremendous grade inflation, and the average for the student body crept to well over 3.0. This is when what Ryan called 'soft classes' started—Black Studies, Women Studies, and so forth.

Ryan remembered finishing his finals and being commissioned on August 24. He'd flown to Los Angeles the next day for his wedding. After he and Claire spent a few days in Las Vegas on their honeymoon, they headed to Ryan's first duty station in the navy, Naval Air Station, North Island in San Diego. He was temporarily "stashed" on the aircraft carrier *Ticonderoga* until his flight-training slot in Pensacola opened up in November. He and Claire lived in a one-bedroom apartment in Coronado—an island-city across San Diego Bay from the main city and accessed by a ferry or a long drive around the southern finger of the Bay. It wasn't until 1969 that a beautiful bridge replaced the ferry.

Ryan and Claire considered Coronado to be a delightful resort and retirement community with the main—indeed only—industry being the navy. Life was good. Ryan spent his days on the ship, ostensibly assigned to the CIC, the combat information center. Since there was no combat, his time was spent drinking coffee and chatting with people on how CIC operated. He met one aviator, an attack jet jock who was part of the ship's company, who asked Ryan what he wanted to fly. Ryan said he was considering helicopters. The man tried to dissuade Ryan. "You'll be spending hours just hovering behind a carrier on plane-guard duty, waiting to pick up some pilot who had to eject because of low fuel or some emergency. Or you'll spend boring time hovering near some suspected submarine with a tethered sonar system dipping in the water. Flying choppers just isn't flying."

He'd been convincing. Ryan scratched helicopters off his list of possibilities. Otherwise, he wandered around the ship talking to people in various stations, including PriFly—the station that monitors all aircrafts' approach to landing. The officers there did enlisted evaluations and otherwise shuffled papers. They were happy to talk to him about carrier operations. He often just went to the wardroom to play chess with other officers in exactly his situation.

On October 22, the ship had just finished a five-day exercise off San Diego and was due in port that night. Around dinnertime, it was announced that all hands were to report to the nearest television. Ryan went to the wardroom and listened to President Kennedy announce a blockade around Cuba because of Soviet missiles in that country. Claire was to meet him on the base but was turned away for security reasons. She was in the dark about the whole story but found out the reason for the delay on TV that night. The ship pulled into port the next day as another carrier left. The reason the *Ticonderoga* couldn't dock that night was because of a policy that said only one carrier could be in one port at any time during a crisis, a long-standing policy left over from World War II.

Before long, Ryan and Claire set off for Pensacola for flight training. It was a fun drive along the southern part of the United States. Things went well until their car started sputtering. Ryan limped into Sulphur, Louisiana, where a perplexed gas station mechanic put a can of Bardahl in the gas tank and told them to try it the next day. They spent the night in a motel and drove twelve miles the next morning to Lake Charles, Louisiana, using a full tank of gas to drive that distance. They found a mechanic who discovered the problem, a leak in the carburetor diaphragm. He replaced it, and they were on their way to Pensacola.

They arrived in the city of navy flight training with less than $100 in hand and about the same amount in the bank. Ryan went to the base to check in and get some back pay. His parents had a friend who had a friend who had arranged for them to look at a beach cottage. They did so and found it perfect. The six cottages in the grouping were all occupied by navy or marine pilot trainees and their wives and were right on the beautiful, white beach by the warm gulf. The rent was $85 a month.

After preflight, he began primary flight training and flight pay of $110 a month came with it. He and Claire blew that amount soon on a three-day trip to New Orleans. The stayed in a nice hotel, went to Preservation Hall to hear some classical jazz, heard the musical greats Pete Fountain and Al Hirt, and dined at Brennans and at the Court of Two Sisters. That amount of money went a long way in those days. Their new adventure had begun.

Chapter Five

All of her days have gone soft and cloudy
All of her dreams have gone dry
All of her nights have gone sad and shady
She's getting ready to fly

—John Denver

IT WAS A BALMY morning in Berlin, and Ryan had the day off. Lexi was in Virginia visiting Camille. He slept late and spent an hour or so updating his flight manual with new approach plate pages. He went out for a stroll with no particular destination in mind. He stopped at a nearby *conditori* for a hard-boiled egg, a *brochen*, and a canned beer. With some concern, he noticed his hands shook as he peeled the egg. Just tired, he supposed. He walked the Tiergarten, the "tiger's playground," Berlin's central park and shopped for some porcelain on *KuDam*. He also managed to admire the topless *fräuleins* sunning in the park. The city was unique to him—it was dynamic, vibrant, and full of faces that reflected optimism and hope. He loved San Francisco and Paris but in different ways. Berlin exuded an eclectic mix of bustle, parks, form, and function. He wandered into a biergarten later for another beer, a Bitburger on tap. Even though he was in a funky mood, he thought the beer was the best he'd ever had. A portly gent who seemed half in the bag asked Ryan where he was from. Ryan told him the United States, and they chatted for a time, somehow getting around to World War II. The German said, "If it wasn't for the damn Jewish problem, the Wehrmacht would have conquered the world."

Ryan certainly didn't want to touch that, so he gulped his beer and tried to get out before he said something he'd regret, but he ultimately couldn't contain himself. "If you were a Hitler admirer, I pity you," he told the old guy. "Do you not, sir, have any sense of history? Think, man. I love the German people. Your country probably has the greatest sense of pride of any culture. You have the best minds for mathematics, philosophy, music, and religion. But forget about reason. Folks can be sheep. Minds are led astray when charismatic leaders lead them to solutions to problems that can be solved by force or dictates, by anything but humanitarianism or reason, dare I say. You know World War I never ended. Germany never ended its quest for dominance in Europe. Minorities, gays, gypsies, Jews, anybody but Aryans were considered animals. And that's how your country, as you knew it, ended. But it has risen from the ashes. Why? Because people who embrace some degree of social egalitarianism, along with free enterprise, are saving you. But, you will note well, with the help of the Marshall Plan, Germany is thriving again, but as a republic. *Gross Gott, mein herr.*"

Ryan cleared his head of that annoying memory and remembered flight training—the days of ground school, primary flight, instruments, aerobatics, and formation flying. The training gave him a mixture of confidence, trepidation, and friendships. Most of Ryan's contemporaries there were broke and scraping by on $222 a month basic pay plus some allowances. Many paid on time for cars, uniforms, and TVs. Nobody had any discretionary money.

Training also involved completing an obstacle course in a

certain time and getting through several rigorous swimming tests. Some wannabe pilots had washed out in that phase, and others had constantly gotten airsick or just decided flying wasn't for them and DORed, dropped on request. The guys who got airsick were told to eat a banana before a flight because it tasted about the same coming up as going down. If that didn't work, they weren't going to make it. Weekends would bring bridge or poker parties with Busch Bavarian beer. They formed solid friendships, and the wives enjoyed talking about starting families and their next duty stations.

Claire and Ryan loved their cottage on Pensacola Beach. Conversations with other pilots involved talking with their hands about aerobatic maneuvers. They discussed what type of aircraft they wanted to fly. Their training took them eventually through night solos, cross-country flying, gunnery, and eventually to aircraft carrier landings. They trained so well for those landings on fixed runways that their first actual carrier landings seemed normal. Ryan recalled that his first solo and his first carrier landings weren't frightening, but the first night solo had been something else. The runway they used had flare pots for runway lighting, and there was no horizon. It was something out of Dante's *Inferno*. But they kept a closed pattern, which meant they made touch-and-go landings with a final full stop. It really had been "white knuckle" flying.

Ryan lost a friend, Rick, a fellow NROTC student in flight training with him, in a drunk-driving accident. He'd unfortunately liquored up at a juke joint near Pensacola and had run into a tree. He was the first loss of a fellow aviator. Ryan recalled that night very well. Rick, Ryan, and two other trainees went to that watering hole to let off some steam. His two friends were former starting football players for Texas Christian University, one a halfback, the other a cornerback. Upon leaving the bar, they were accosted by three toughs who looked pretty buff. They said something like, "You're pretty special, you guys. But you can't handle the real world—can't get the chicks. You think you can get all the girls you want—well you can't."

"Back off, guys. We don't want this, and you don't either," Ryan said.

"You folks got yourselves into this, acting like you're special. Let's see what you have," came a taunt.

"We didn't do anything. We're walking out of here. If you want to stop us, go ahead." Ryan was in shape, as they all were, but not in fighting shape. Rick was about like Ryan. They could outrun them all, but where would they be then? What would the word on the street be? So Ryan rather irrationally asked, "What do you guys want?"

"Try this, flyboy." One threw a right at Ryan, which he blocked with his left forearm and answered with a right cross to the guy's chin. Ryan threw him over his hip and sat on him, hitting him in the nose if he tried anything. Ryan hadn't dominated him; he'd just landed a lucky blow. His two TCU buddies threw combinations that put the other two guys down to stay, and then they pummeled them. Rick just held his own, making sure the three were down to stay down. They called the police from the bar. Ryan didn't know what ultimately happened to the thugs and didn't care; he was just grateful that they'd learned some judo and self-defense in preflight. Rick, however, drove away in his own car that night and met his sad fate.

Another good friend from college who had also been in the NROTC program simply couldn't adapt to flying and dropped out. Ryan experienced this second loss as he progressed through the program; he always remembered the guy well. Two of the remaining close friends who had been in that fight went to bars occasionally, much to the chagrin of their wives, but they went only a couple of times a month. Time was precious, but they had to let off steam—and it was part of the program, wasn't it?

They had one week of survival training at Eglin Air Force Base in Florida. It was actually five days of navigating piney woods to a particular destination. They had no food for the entire period except for one day, when about twenty of them caught an owl and several flying squirrels. They cleaned those, mixed the grilled meat with some reindeer moss, added some boiling water, and they each consumed about a half-cup of calories.

They conducted primary and basic flight training over Georgia and eastern Alabama. They were taught that if they were lost to remember the four Cs: Climb for better radio range, Conserve by getting a leaner fuel-air mixture to increase endurance, Confess that they were really lost, and Call on Guard frequency that they were disoriented; someone would probably respond, and vectors were possible. Ground stations could monitor radio transmissions and provide directional steers. This situation was not uncommon, and the solution was to be calm and rational.

Eventually, most of them went to advanced training in Corpus Christi, Texas. When Ryan checked in at operations there, he was asked what he wanted to fly, jets or multiengine. His grades had been good, so he had a choice. They more or less pushed jets since Vietnam was just heating up, but at that point Ryan was truly unsure. He knew from his midshipman cruises that he didn't like ships. The thought of flying jets off and onto a carrier for six months or more and being away from his family was not appealing even if the macho part was. Being a jet jockey was hot stuff. On the other hand, many of them had talked about airline flying. The pay was great, it was a chance to travel, it was prestigious, and the work usually involved being off duty about two weeks a month. He told the operations officer to give him a couple of hours to consider the decision. He and Claire went to the base cafeteria for breakfast and weighed the pros and cons. They decided flying multiengine was the best path to airline flying and would minimize their separations. Also, by flying multiengine, he could take his family with him on deployments as he would be land based.

As Ryan's memories flashed by, he realized that had been the best decision of his life. If he'd flown jets off a carrier, he would have made at least two nine-month deployments to the Pacific and would have flown countless missions over North Vietnam. Looking back, he remembered how many friends he'd lost over 'Nam and several who had been imprisoned for years. Of course he'd lost friends through routine training flights or other operational missions, as he had told Kate. He realized he was very lucky to have had a full career in naval aviation and to have achieved the rank of captain. He recalled Dieter Dengler, who got his wings about the same time as Ryan; Dengler had been shot down over Laos during the war. He was held captive for weeks, escaped, and was picked up by an American helicopter, the first American military man to escape captivity in that theater. Ryan knew he could have been in Dengler's situation.

Ryan remembered an extremely interesting trip to Iwakuni, Japan with his squadron in '64. He was at the officers' club bar watching the Olympic Games, which were being held in Tokyo. Among the entrants in the final ten-thousand-meter run was Billy Mills, a young US Marine first lieutenant who was part Sioux. He was a long shot in this race, the favorite being Ron Clarke of Australia, who held the world's record at this distance. In the final lap, Clarke was boxed in and nudged Mills. Then both were pushed by Mohammed Gammoudi of Tunisia. Mills and Clarke stumbled slightly, and then Mills moved outside to lane three and sprinted home to win the gold, beating his own best time by fifty seconds and setting a new Olympic record. In that Marine officers' club with about a hundred or more officers watching this amazing feat, all the navy and marine folks went into a wild frenzy. They went crazy, throwing glasses all around. Ryan had always loved watching all Olympic events, but that race had been the most memorable he had seen or probably ever would see in Olympic competition.

He thought about some of the most interesting airports he'd flown into. The approach into Kai Tak airport in Hong Kong was very challenging. Although the runway, 3,390 meters was long, when landing toward Victoria Harbor, there was no overrun. The normal approach was through the city, and there were six-story buildings to the north. Pilots could see laundry hanging on balconies and flickering television sets in apartment buildings as they approached.

The landing at the Coast Guard Station in Kodiak, Alaska was even more challenging. The main approach was over the water to a runway 7,542 feet long, plenty long, but the problem was the hills on three sides, each several hundred feet high. If a plane was below five hundred feet as it approached, the pilot could not wave off—he simply didn't have the time or power to clear those hills, so below that altitude, landings were mandatory. There were numerous crosses planted in the hills to demarcate planes that had crashed over the years.

The most nerve-wracking approach in aviation had to be into Saigon's Ton Son Nhut airport at the height of the war. The main runway's length was not a problem, but at one time it was the world's busiest airport. It had to be approached with a four-and-a-half degree glide slope, half again steeper than normal, to minimize damage from ground fire. This sometimes necessitated opening the bomb bay doors for more drag to increase the rate descent. The airport had helicopters constantly approaching from various directions—attack birds, medevac helos, and supply flights. Plus, the takeoffs and landings included a wide variety of fixed-wing aircraft, including fighter and attack planes, cargo planes, charter flights from various airlines such as Pan Am, Northwest, and World Airways, observation aircraft, and various other birds. The squadron always parked in revetments (sandbagged walls on three sides) to minimize damage from mortars. Crewmembers wore survival vests and Mae West life preservers in weather that was invariably terribly hot and humid. He recalled times when he would hear a medevac helicopter telling the tower that it needed a brain surgeon upon landing. He had nightmares about that experience for years after.

As Ryan walked the streets of Berlin, which he'd grown very fond of, he noticed the people, the smells, and the architecture. It was really a "green" city. The people walked with purpose, and the parks smelled of cedar, pine, and grass—freshness permeated the air. The buildings were built for function more than style—at least in Ryan's mind. He and Lexi didn't have a car in Berlin because the public transportation was so good. He walked by the Kaiser Wilhelm *Kirche;* the fabled church still bore pockmarks from shelling during the war.

Then he had the panicky thought—*Am I supposed to fly today?* He took out his monthly schedule from his wallet and saw the day was indeed free. *Am I cracking up? Is all this flying and the monthly trips to the United States starting to stress me out? Pull yourself together, Ryan. Get a grip.* He decided another Bitburger would calm him down. He went back to the apartment for a nap, watched a little TV, and went out for a pizza Margherita. There wasn't much traffic as he walked home that night, but the disciplined Germans didn't walk at pedestrian crossings if the red "no walking" light was on, cars or not.

When Lexi returned to Berlin, it was business as usual. Ryan would fly a few days and have a few days off. They took one interesting trip to Oslo via Frankfurt and London, and they loved Oslo, where they stayed in a nice downtown hotel. They walked down to the fjord waterfront and had a couple of beers and a pizza. The bill came to about $50. Oslo was not cheap, nor were any of the other Nordic countries.

Over dinner, after he'd worked up the courage with a few beers, he told Lexi he'd met an interesting flight attendant. "Oh, really?" she replied. "Why's she interesting?"

"Well, don't get the wrong idea. You know me better than that. It's just that she's American—the only flight attendant in Berlin from America. Her father's an executive with Contrails and got her a job with the company, so she's working here to get a feel for operations. She went to Stanford and got an MBA from Wharton. That's how we got to talking at a crew dinner. We had a couple of things in common—you know, the school, sports, San Francisco, business. You'll like her. She's down to earth, no pretenses, a lot like you."

"I see. Well, I trust you. You've never cheated on me, and you've had countless chances. Pardon me while I turn off this mental alarm bell."

"You got that right. About never cheating, I mean. And opportunities as well, of course. But this is strictly platonic, naturally. She's just interesting, that's all."

"Is she pretty? Contrails doesn't hire plain women."

"I suppose you could call her pretty. Well, some have mentioned her as being attractive. Something like that. Not ordinary. Mainly smart and nice, like you, so to speak."

"Yes, I do know you. We've been together for almost five years, you naïve *dummkopf*."

"Don't call me naïve, *mein schatze*."

"Okay, just *dummkopf.* You're not a snob, but you don't fuss much over average women. I believe you. I look forward to meeting her. When will that be?"

"Oh, soon, I'd guess. She flies all the routes over here, including those to the Eastern Bloc, so it could be on any flight. We can have dinner together, the three of us, right?"

"Not with the whole crew?"

"Well, maybe that. We'll see what happens. You'd get to know her better if it was just the three of us."

"Why do I want to get to know her better? There are a couple of hundred flight attendants over here."

"Well, she lives in Berlin. If you hit it off, you could do things together. You have no friends here."

"I have you. That's enough. We're always together. But she lives in Berlin? Where? Have you ever seen her here?"

"She lives in an apartment near Grunewald in the Dahlem area with two other flight attendants. And no, I've never seen her in this city—that would be dating. I wouldn't do that."

"That's a very upscale area. But you've been with her in other places, right?"

"Right, but not what you would call dates per se. I would call them … discussions … seminars. I just thought … well, never mind. That's enough about her."

"What a crock! Listen, this is a dangerous situation. I'm sure dining with a beautiful woman is more fun than being with the whole crew, but put me on record for being against this situation. I can't stop you. Do as you wish, but you're on thin ice, and if something happens I'll know it. That's enough for now."

"I have something else to tell you."

"You want a divorce."

"Don't be ridiculous. I've been noticing tremors in my right hand. And sometimes I get dizzy. At times my balance isn't right. I'm a little concerned."

"That, of course, could be a lot of things. How long has this been going on?"

"A few months. I guess we'll watch it for a while, and if it gets worse, I'll get it checked in the States. Trouble is, I have to report all my doctor visits on my annual FAA physical. Maybe I'll just check informally with my old flight surgeon friend."

"Well, it's a concern. But as you say, we'll watch it and get it checked out soon."

The next morning they had a complimentary breakfast of the usual Scandinavian dishes—pickled herring, sausages, cheeses, boiled eggs, and hash. When the crew met in the lobby, the captain was frantic. He said, "My uniform and passport are missing. I looked all over." The pilots told the front desk the story, and the captain went with them to the airport in civilian clothes. He told the station manager to wire Berlin that he would be arriving with no passport and for them to get him entry clearance. They took off and received a message en route that the hotel had found the captain's items in a closet in his room. The cockpit crew had large rooms, and the captain had simply failed to check all his closets. Embarrassing but humorous.

A couple of days later they had a pattern that took them from Frankfurt to Zagreb, Yugoslavia, for a layover. The fateful day had come; Lexi was going to meet Katarina, but that wouldn't come until they were on the crew bus to the hotel. Lexi and Ryan flew together on almost every trip, except when Lexi was in the States checking on their condo in San Diego and or visiting her sister in Virginia. Ryan flew with Kate at least once a month, but as the relationship got closer, they tried to bid the patterns that would give them more trips together. But for this first meeting, on the shuttle to the hotel for the flight crew, Lexi and Ryan sat together, and Kate, with a goofy grin on her face, sat next to them across the aisle. He said, "Lexi, this is Katarina, or K ...K ... Kate. Kate, meet my wife, Lexi."

They shook hands and exchanged pleasantries. They talked about never having been in Zagreb and about going out for dinner.

"What about the crew?" Lexi asked.

"Screw the crew," Ryan said. "I mean, I think we should talk and get to know each other. I'm hungry for Croatian food."

"What's Croatian food?" Lexi asked. "We don't have Croatian restaurants in America."

"Of course we do, in, ah, Croatian areas," Ryan answered. "Somewhere. They probably specialize in seafood, maybe moussaka or something, being near the Adriatic. I've heard there's an Italian influence in Croatian food. Probably Greek dishes too."

At that point, Ryan supposed his blood pressure was around 200 over 120, but after they got their hotel rooms and freshened up, they met in the lobby and set out on the search for wonderful Croatian food. They engaged in small talk during the stroll. Kate mentioned she had chatted with someone, a bellhop maybe, while waiting in the lobby and had learned there was a lot of enmity between Serbs and Croats that apparently went back for centuries due to a long-forgotten *casus belli*.

The trio found a nice restaurant and scanned the menu. No kabobs in sight, but plenty of seafood. They settled on a whole broiled sea bass, fresh vegetables, and a white wine. Then came the crunch Ryan had been waiting for as he fiddled with his napkin. His hands shook as he tested the wine. Lexi was not unobservant; she sensed the existing emotional undercurrent, but she kicked it off. "Ryan says you went to Stanford and have an MBA from Wharton. I went to the University of Virginia and loved it there.

"Are you dating anyone, Kate?" Lexi asked.

"I was until recently, but travel's hard on a relationship. My boyfriend lived in Silicon Valley. You two are so lucky you're able to be together on most flights. Someday I'll find someone when the time is right, and I'll marry. I had friends that went to the University of Virginia. It's a great school founded by Thomas Jefferson."

"I thought of Dartmouth and USC," Ryan said, "but my conversations with high school mentors and my research led me to Stanford. No regrets. I had the NROTC scholarship, which prohibited me from getting married, but it paid all the tuition, books, and fees. This was before the Vietnam War. During that war, ROTC was dismantled in various great universities because of the protests in America. During the war, NROTC was done away with at many places, and that was the end of the program at Stanford—protestors burned the building. MIT, Harvard, and others lost ROTC too."

"Well, anyhow, we all went to good schools," Kate said. "Stanford, Wharton, and Virginia. It's nice you two have something special. That's enviable. I hope to have a marriage like yours someday."

She wants to marry—that's intriguing! Ryan thought, but he recovered quickly and made some inane remark about the right person coming along for sure. "You have so much to offer. When you are ready you'll find the perfect person." Interesting conversation flowed well among the three intelligent people. Ryan wondered if Lexi was uncomfortable or if she suspected considerable chemistry was percolating in his relationship with Kate. He felt tense, but Lexi seemed to have no problem keeping the conversation flowing.

"Where's home for you in America?" Lexi asked.

"We live in Atherton, by Palo Alto. I love the Bay Area—can't imagine living anywhere else."

Lexi offered that San Diego was nice, as was Seattle, except for the rain. She said Ryan had been stationed in Monterey for a couple of years, an area they loved as well. The rest of the dinner went along with no major gaffes. They walked back to the hotel with only quiet conversation and said their goodnights in the lobby.

Back in their room, Ryan asked Lexi, "Well that went rather well, don't you think?"

"Yes, she is charming. It was fun to get to know her. You said she wasn't ordinary. She's flawless! Stunning and nice. It's a good thing I'm not the jealous type or there might be a big worry."

"Well, she's a good person, but she's not perfect. Anyway, you're my true love, as you know."

"In what way is she imperfect? How do you know that?"

"She told me so. There must be skeletons or something. Actually, she once had a speech impediment—stuttering. She got over it. Anyhow, she's not my type."

"She speaks perfectly. And she's lovely—you never actually said that, right? Don't answer. I already know. You're forgiven—for something; I'm just not sure of what."

Lexi and Kate, Kate and Lexi. I have a tiger by the tail. What happens now? he thought.

CHAPTER SIX

Silver wings
Shining in the sunlight.
Roaring engines
Heading somewhere in flight
—Garrett Hedlund

LEXI ACCOMPANIED RYAN ON one particular flight from Frankfurt to Budapest, about an hour and forty-five minutes away, and then on to the captivating city of Dubrovnik, Yugoslavia, a flight of a little over an hour. The pilots met the flight attendants in operations, where the paperwork was filled out. Al Hartman was the captain, and Petra was part of the team, of course. Al briefed the cabin crew, and they departed. The first leg was routine. Ryan would be making the landing at Dubrovnik, his second in this lovely, historic, walled city. On his first trip there, he had toured the shops and sights within the walls. It was said that Richard the Lion Hearted came to this city for rest and recreation during the Crusades. The weather was fine, but the runway had an uphill slope, which usually made for a challenging landing because the runway came up to meet a plane a little earlier than most pilots were used to. The landing was a little hard, so as they taxied in, Ryan felt compelled to say, "Folks, this is the first officer. That landing was a little rough. I made the landing, but it wasn't my fault. It also wasn't the plane's fault or the company's fault. It was the asphalt." Perhaps there were enough English-speaking people on board to get the lame joke.

They cleared customs and immigration and got on the crew bus to their hotel, where, as usual in Eastern Bloc countries, they turned in their passports to get room keys. Ryan and Lexi loved Dubrovnik, a walled city on the banks of the Adriatic. They changed, shopped, and walked a couple of blocks downhill to the seafront, where they enjoyed seafood and a nice local wine.

"This is an enchanting spot," Ryan said. "Lexi, we are blessed to fly to these exotic places together. These memories will last together. But I want to tell you something which is rather sensitive. I fly with Kate on about every ninth or tenth flight. I know you like her. Do you really understand I like to dine with her on certain layovers when you're away? Of course, you're with us often on many of these trips. But does it *really* bother you if she and I meet and talk and have meals together? She and I have never been here in Dubrovnik together. I realize there's the appearance of volatility, but we just really get along well. It seems the three of us are all good friends. Dining with the whole crew gets frenetic."

"She's a very nice person, hon. I trust you to not get carried away, although it's still a dangerous situation. It seems we're all simpatico. It's okay because I like her, but I'm still uncomfortable. Just let me know what goes on. Be honest with me."

A couple of weeks later, Lexi was in Virginia while Ryan was first officer of a charter from Frankfurt to Pula and Split, in Croatia, Yugoslavia. Croatia again, and Kate was working the flight. They flew for a couple of hours to Pula, where about half the passengers got off to see the Roman ruins and explore the wonders of the Adriatic coast. The pilots filed some clearance papers and flew a short leg to Split, in the northwest corner of Croatia.

Split was a wonderful resort city where the Roman emperor Diocletian had built a palace. The city's historic center is among the United Nations' World Heritage sites. The beautiful town, in the foothills of the Dalmatian mountains, boasted a wonderful climate: hot, dry summers, and mild, wet winters. The crew headed to a first-class hotel. After Ryan and Katarina changed in their respective rooms, they met discreetly at a bar a block from the hotel. Katarina had told her flight attendant roommate she would not meet the crew for dinner because she wanted to grab a quick bite and catch up on her reading in a quiet place. Ryan had made a similar excuse to his fellow cockpit crewmembers.

The two had a brief conversation after passing through customs and had picked out a bar on the way to the hotel. They walked from their rendezvous to a nice restaurant in the old town, right by the Adriatic, where they ate *soparnik*, a dough filled with vegetables and baked on a fireplace, and *cevapi*, grilled minced meat rolls with onions and peppers, and a good white wine. His hand shook slightly as he raised his glass. "We both made excuses for not dining with the crew, right?" Ryan asked.

"Yes. Mine was rather lame. But your hand is trembling."

"I guess I'm a little nervous, Kate. This type of thing is new to me—new since we met. I'd like to pay you a compliment, but I don't want you take it the wrong way."

"Shoot. Girls like compliments."

He opened his mouth to speak, but nothing came out. He regrouped and tried again. "Well, I'd like to say you're put together quite well. You stay in good shape. Do you work out often? How do you do that, given our schedules?"

"Thank you. I try to run in the Grunewald in Berlin, and sometimes I work out at layover hotels. I don't count calories, but mentally I try to stay at around eighteen hundred or so a day."

"Actually, you have breathtaking beauty. You have kindness, vitality, and intellect, the whole package. That's rare."

"I think perhaps you're judgmental about beauty."

Ryan's face hardened as he said, "Hey! You said you'd been in some beauty pageant. But let me rephrase that. I appreciate beauty. Who doesn't? I admit to turning my head when I see a gorgeous woman. Isn't that normal? But in my heart I know character is more important than beauty."

Kate was somewhat chastened. "Right. I'll get to that contest. But I believe in excellence. I don't read a book if it doesn't stimulate my mind. I don't listen to a song if it doesn't lift my spirits or send me a message. I won't watch a film if it doesn't stir my emotions. I think we agree we don't settle for mediocrity. But thank you. You said some nice words, but you lay it on pretty heavy, kind sir."

"Well, all are true. I imagine hundreds of guys lined up to hit on you or ask you out in high school, college, and grad school. Did you have any serious relationships?"

"I'm a normal woman with normal desires and drives. Yes, I dated fairly often but never had any serious relationships. Nothing ever clicked. My studies were my first priority."

"Couldn't find Mr. Right, huh?"

"I suppose my standards are high. I do want a family someday. I'd be looking for qualities you attributed to me, although I'm far from perfect, as I told you once before."

"Could have fooled me. But the right person will come along, as karma will have it. You ever hear, 'Things will be all right in the end. If things aren't all right, it's not the end.'? I wonder, do you think a man can love two women at the same time, or vice versa?"

"Love is a relative word. It comes in many forms. You love your father in one way and your brother in another. You'd love two children equally but differently."

"Do you think infidelity is a sin?" he asked.

"Boy, you speak in vague, relative, ambiguous terms. You might as well ask me if I believe in abortion or capital punishment. What's a sin anyway? A white lie is still a lie, but at times it's appropriate. A doctor may tell someone that his or her spouse died peacefully, when in fact there was great suffering at the end. The words may ease emotional grief. Adultery is a crime, but are all crimes immoral? If a poor man steals a loaf of bread to feed his family, is that immoral? If a man's unfaithful once, is there harm if the spouse never knows? Sure, guilt is a heavy burden. Sin, morality, and crime are man-made constructs, but they keep society orderly. Laws prevent anarchy. But I suppose we all can justify behavior or actions without the consideration of morality."

"Well, lying isn't one of the seven deadly sins—pride, greed, anger, lust, envy, gluttony, and sloth."

"But it does violate the Ten Commandments."

"Point taken. But I think yes and no answers come hard for you. Your nuanced speech is endearing."

"And you're a good conversationalist. That's endearing as well. I don't like to talk about physical beauty, but all right, maybe you should know I was first runner-up in the Miss California beauty contest about nine years ago. My parents kind of pushed me into it. Now I think it's a rather vacuous endeavor."

"The judges must have been visually impaired to select you

as a runner-up. You never stop amazing me, but, okay, we'll change the subject."

"One more thing on the Miss California issue. I think in that type of thing there are politics, favorites, negotiations, perhaps even payoffs. It probably operates like the International Olympic Committee. Anyhow, the winner nailed a Cole Porter song in the talent part, while I jumped around doing a modern dance routine. I thought about singing, but I really wasn't that good. I could do modern dancing, though. But who cares about that? She got points there. What are your likes and dislikes?"

"I don't care for loud, aggressive people. They're just vexing. I knew some in the navy. Or swearing. Or improper use of grammar, such as dangling prepositions, the misuse of 'I' and 'me' or 'we' and 'us,' or "you know" too often. Those things are just abrasive to me. I guess I'm somewhat of a perfectionist. And probably somewhat narcissistic."

"No, narcissism is pretending to be someone you're not—puffing yourself up. Don't confuse that with good grooming, dressing well, and carrying yourself well."

"In other words, it isn't bragging if you can do it. I think Yogi Berra may have said that—not sure. He once said nobody goes to a certain restaurant anymore because it's too crowded."

"Funny. But you're not narcissistic."

"I like sports—especially golf now—reading, travel, painting—watercolors mainly. I like music—pop, classical, country. But I found I have no talent for playing an instrument, and I certainly can't sing. I love good movies. I suppose *Casablanca, Ben Hur,* and *Dr. Zhivago* were my favorites. What are your likes? Don't tell me sunsets and walks along the beach," Ryan said.

"Those are all love stories. Ryan, you're a romantic!"

"Yes. I'm a hopeless romantic. My feelings run deep."

"Well, I pretty much like life. I like the challenge of a

new day. I like learning and travel. Meeting people, trying not to judge them. Tennis, of course. I'm an Ayn Rand fan. I strongly believe in free enterprise. Hard work and innovation should be rewarded. Companies succeed or fail depending on how they meet demand. Good companies grow, reward their shareholders, hire more people, and expand the economy and the tax base. There should be a safety net for the disadvantaged, but I believe in equal opportunity, not equal outcome. I dislike socialism—it stifles economic growth. I've seen plenty of that in Eastern Europe. I like small government and low taxes. People who don't pay taxes have representation without taxation—the opposite of how our country was founded. I believe all wage earners should pay some income tax—even those who make minimum wage. Those folks could pay just one percent, say, up to twenty grand, and maybe a marginal rate of three percent up to thirty grand, and then it would be progressive upward. That way every worker would have skin in the game; they'd have a greater interest and understanding of tax policy and how taxes are used.

"I believe in trickle-down economics, but I'm not too keen on trickle-up poverty. Public education is a function of the states, and they should give it the highest priority to help people better themselves. Our country will never be destroyed from the outside, but it could rot from within."

"Yes, America is not the same as it was during the decade in which I went to high school and when you were born," Ryan said. "And the change isn't for the better."

"*Das ist der zeitgeist,*" Kate said. "Things are as they are. We can't change society. We can only try to live our lives in ways that contribute in a small way to the betterment of all."

"So you speak German on top of everything else."

"My ancestors came from Bavaria. My grandparents spoke German and English. I picked up German early and took it in school. There's some French in the mix too. My maternal great grandmother was born in Marseilles."

"It's interesting that you're a conservative in her midtwenties. Conventional wisdom says if you're not a liberal in your twenties, you don't have a heart, and if you're not a conservative after age forty, you don't have a brain. The great philosopher, Muhammad Ali—also a pretty good boxer—said, 'The man who views the world at fifty the same as he did at twenty has wasted thirty years of his life.' Actually, I try to live by several rules. Don't lie. Don't cheat. Be true to your word. Always do your best. Mean what you say. Never assume. Don't take things personally."

"Boy, if you can follow those, you should be the president or a saint," Katarina said.

"I'm no saint, and I fail to follow those often, but those thoughts guide me. They're helpful."

"Well I'm no saint either," came Katarina's reply. "I don't follow the herd mentality. I think for myself, keep my own counsel, and formed my political opinions rather early on. Plus my parents were conservative."

"Do you embrace any organized religion?"

"No, I'm pretty much secular and rational. And you?"

"The same. I brook no dogma, but I'm spiritual in some ways. There's some prime power or mover. I can't make a tree. What started the Big Bang? I don't know what follows death. Sometimes I think all I've ever known is life, and that's all I'll ever know in some form. Or maybe what follows death is what there was before life—nothing. I suppose I'm agnostic, although I don't like that term. A pragmatist or an objectivist maybe. I've heard it said the only true measurement of intelligence is whether you can live happily. Do you embrace that notion?"

"No. Intellect and happiness are not mutually exclusive or inclusive. Intellect is probably largely inherited, whereas knowledge and wisdom are learned. Happiness is more of an indication of a well-adjusted mind or good emotional health. You can be smart and happy or smart and miserable. Anyhow, I think you create the conditions of your own existence. What do you think?"

"I think happiness is a moment. I think Marcel Proust said something about the anticipation and the remembrance being better than the experience. Contentment is more enduring. I'm content, but I've had many happy moments."

"Such as?"

"Getting my driver's license, scoring twenty points in a basketball game, my weddings, my first A in calculus, getting my naval aviator wings, my first carrier landing, having my children and watching them develop well, and so many more. In 1978, I was transferred from Naval Air Station, Moffett Field, California, to the Pentagon. My kids were preteens. My first wife and I bought a used Volkswagen Westphalia—the pop-up camper. We drove to Vancouver and across Canada on the Trans-Canada highway and down to Virginia. We'd camp one night and stay in a hotel the next. It was a wonderful trip as we listened to Abba, John Denver, and Neil Diamond tapes much of the way. In Canada, the wonderful campgrounds were not crowded, and elk would wander into our camping area. We could see Rocky Mountain sheep along the way. We were all happy the entire trip.

"Much of my education has emphasized optimization. Maximizing profits, creating the perfect investment portfolio, designing an excellent missile, making perfect landings. Sometimes I think the concept of 'satisficing' is more important. It's more expedient and less apt to frustrate. Pilots always want to make a perfect landing. Can't be done, but the passengers expect it. Actually, any landing you walk away from is okay. In aircraft carrier landings, you always try to catch the third wire out of four. But as long as you get aboard, it's satisfactory. A safe carrier landing is redundant, although pilots are graded on their landings. I believe the single most demanding endeavor in existence is making a night carrier landing in rough seas. It takes total concentration, coordination, nerves, and a certain amount of smarts. Perhaps maneuvering a landing module for a lunar touchdown surpasses that. But there have been no fatalities in lunar landings, and countless in carrier landings. Of course, the databases contrast markedly."

"I agree with that," Katarina offered, "but can't identify with it. But I admire pioneers, innovators, and superb athletes. I think the single greatest achievement in sports is winning Olympic gold in the decathlon. When you win that medal, you're called 'the world's greatest athlete.' It takes speed, strength, coordination, and endurance. But, of course, great achievements don't necessarily make great human beings."

"Yes, Bob Mathias from Stanford won that medal twice—in 1948 and 1952. Truly a remarkable achievement. He went on to become a congressman, and I think he was well regarded. Working at the Pentagon for six years probably helped me achieve a higher rank. Thank God there was a nice gym in the biggest office building in the world. Every day, whether it was a hundred degrees or freezing, I'd change and run four miles. I had routes marked out. I'd run to the Jefferson Memorial, down the Potomac to National Airport, to the Marine Memorial, or to Georgetown. That was the only way to keep my sanity. The last three years I served as a senior budget analyst with constant deadlines and had to provide quick answers to congressional staffers. It helped my career but probably took a year off my life. Some officers have said the best sight in the world is the Pentagon out your rear-view window.

"I told you before, Kate, I was divorced once. We were young and very happy, went through much of the navy together, and had two fine children—Todd and Pam. The first is at William and Mary, the second at the University of Virginia, and they're both good kids."

"Well, they're going to fine schools."

"Yes, and our divorce agreement included no alimony—she got the house, we split some assets, and I'm paying for college, but it's in-state tuition. Claire is a vice president at a sports clothing firm. She got an advanced degree at George Mason while I was at the Pentagon. I worked late, she studied late, we lost our traditional holiday getaways, and, well, we just grew apart. She's a fine person. We just stopped communicating, except about the kids. I guess you could say love had run its course. Things like that don't have to happen, but they do. Her work was important to her. She had a need to self-actualize, and I had to climb the military ladder. I worked late, but I tried to help the kids. I guess marriage took hind seat. And she wanted no part of my next military change of station. So we agreed to part. I met Lexi, we dated about a year before we married, and now we have a condo in San Diego."

"I'm sorry about the divorce. Anytime you want to talk about it more, here I am."

They were done with the mundane. The exchange of ideas took deeper forms. The ambiance was enchanting. They talked of school years, college experiences, values, hopes, and dreams as the sun turned orange-gold and dipped below the horizon. They were quiet for a while.

"Sometimes I dream, but I try to live in the moment," Ryan said. "I know my life is as complete as anyone's can be."

"Someday, I know, the right man will appear for me," Kate replied. "I imagine he'll be a lot like you."

"I'm not good enough for you, Kate. I'm not in your league."

"You are, Ryan, you are. More correctly, you're in a league

of your own. I've always been strong in my resolve and sense of responsibility, but lately I've been somewhat befuddled. I don't know what's going on. For the first time in my life I feel breakable."

"I think you've had enough of flying," Ryan said. "Living out of a suitcase is taxing. You aren't cut out to be a flight attendant. The job can grind you down with all the sameness. It's time to move on. But I also have those feelings of being out of kilter. I know I'm getting sick in some way, but this angst is more emotional. Kate, I'm not a philanderer. I have a divorce, a new wife, and here you are. What does that make me?"

"Ryan, you're a fine person. You feel, you do emote, and that's rare in men. Maybe that's why I like you. But about your job, isn't it routine also?"

"Hardly. The only constants are the checklists and where the gauges and switches are. Every airport is different, the weather always changes, and we have to be constantly thinking about fuel, alternates, and safety. Anyhow, Claire said I didn't emote enough."

"For me, it's not the job, although I'm ready for change, it's about feelings. Something's going on here."

"I think we have a mutual admiration society. Kate, we've talked about a lot things and have gotten to know each other, but maybe we should drop pretenses. Let's walk back and talk about these feelings. I need to tell you what can be and what can never be."

They spent several hours in Ryan's room, sipping on some cognac he'd purchased in Frankfurt. They talked some more with moments of stillness. They were aware of a growing fondness between them but also of boundaries that could not be crossed. *Or could they?* Somewhere a bell tolled midnight. They knew they'd have to be in the lobby in several hours for the flight. Gradually the evening ended in the most tender way.

Ryan said, "You know, dear girl, this can ... this will never ... maybe all this can be ..."

"Is a sweet memory that passes through our minds from time to time," came Katarina's soft response.

"Maybe, in another world, another time ..."

"For all sad words of tongue and pen, the saddest are these, 'It might have been.'"

"Who wrote that? I've heard it before."

"John Greenleaf Whittier. But remember, the Talmud says something about a person being called into account on Judgment Day for every permissible thing he might have enjoyed but did not."

"Kate, for me you're kind of the road not taken. I don't mean this to be more than it is, but when I look into those emerald eyes, I can see forever."

"Ah, you speak of Robert Frost. And maybe you go too far. Don't beat yourself up. Your life is predictable. You and Lexi will probably have kids, and you'll be happy watching your children and grandchildren grow. So maybe you shouldn't reach for something beyond your grasp. You'll play ball with all those kids and travel with Lexi and grow old gracefully together. It'll be a good life."

"And you'll find the right man to spend your life with, but you can't cull the wheat from the chaff unless you see people. Date and date some more until you find someone who's right for you. For me, Lexi's my life. She complements me and makes me whole. I can't imagine, without letting my imagination run wild, living my life now without her. But you've really stirred some deep feelings within me, and you'll always be in my dream world."

"I think I understand you and know the real you. You're a great catch. I would like to be friends with you forever. Who knows in what way?"

"Honesty is an act of grace," Ryan said. "Temptation isn't tempting. But I guess I don't believe that. That doesn't make sense, and it's not honest. Kate, I just can't find the words. These feelings can't be spoken. Kate, it pains me to say this, but if I want a solid marriage with Lexi, which I do, I have to be honest with her. You and I have become emotionally involved—probably beyond what's proper. Our relationship's on the brink of being uncontrollable. I think we should stop trying to bid patterns that put us together. Lexi has to travel to Virginia often. Let's just bid for places and patterns we like. I have to go back to trying to have a week off at the end of one month and a week off at the start of the next. We'll fly together randomly, maybe occasionally dine together alone, but we have to cool this thing down."

"Sadly, I know you're right," Kate said. "But it's not as though we're parting. That would be beyond sad."

Ryan knew they would fly together and dine together from time to time, and the flame would merely smolder, never igniting. *Or would it?* He wondered.

Not long later, the two were paired again on a pattern. Loading began in Heathrow for a flight to Frankfurt—a continuation of a flight from Oslo. The passenger boarding was a little early, so Ryan had a few minutes to step into the first class galley to grab a cup of coffee. He took a sip and then almost spilled the whole cup as he spied a woman he knew well coming through the front cabin door. She saw him at the same time. He sputtered, "Claire, what on earth are you doing here?"

"Hello, Ryan. What a nice surprise! I thought there might be an off chance of catching you aboard. I'm on my way to a conference and to meet with some buyers of our new sporting line. I already spent a few days in Stockholm. You know, with

Steffi Graff and Boris Becker, all the Germans are really getting into tennis in a big way. The Swedes are coming on strong in tennis and golf too—Edberg, Borg, and so forth. How do they do that with those long winters? What a market over here! I may go to Spain as well—not sure about that yet. And they want fancy outfits too, except for when they play in Wimbledon, of course. The players there must wear mainly white while on the court. We have some fine lines of clothes, and the prices are reasonable. I stayed a few days at the crew hotel where you lay over—I was planning to stay there thinking you'd be passing through one of these days, and here you are. It's great to see you! I don't suppose you're up for dinner tonight?"

"No ... I mean yes, that is, of course, well ... it's complicated. But it's so nice to see you too. And a real shock. Dinner would be nice. I mean ... it's obligatory ... no ... I mean of course I want to ... yes ... certainly. You see, there's a little snag. I'm married now, as you know, and Lexi is aboard. She's here, in first class. I'll introduce you, and you two can make some plans. And, ah, there's a sticky wicket here, you might say. Lexi and I are both good friends with a flight attendant—Kate. She's serving in first class. We're all friends, so we can work something out."

What a revoltin' development, Ryan thought. *I have some 'splaining to do. This is uncharted territory, a regular three-ring circus, and I'm the ringleader.*

"Oh, I see. A threesome or a foursome. I didn't know you had it in you Ryan."

"Don't be silly—it's nothing like that. Well, it's complicated, but we'll all get along and sort things out. Anyhow, are you happy, Claire?"

"Very much. I love my job, and I'm dating a bit."

"Very glad to hear that."

It should be a memorable evening, Ryan thought. *Memorable as hell.*

After they had checked in to the hotel, the four walked to a nice German restaurant near the hotel. After the menus had been perused, Claire said, "I'll have the *weener snitzel*, please."

Kate said, "That's a good German dish. *Wienerschnitzel.* You may not know German food well, Claire. It's wonderful, but we pronounce it *veener schnitzel.* See the distinction? Germans pronounce the *w* like a *v*, and you have to hear the *sh* sound in schnitzel. German really isn't complicated. They have long words, though nothing like the Finns."

"Well, Sweden was fun with their language."

"Most Swedes our ages," Kate offered, "speak English. It's very important to them to look them in the eye when you toast."

Ryan decided to jump in. "Please pass the salt, Claire."

Claire said, "Never salt without tasting, Ryan. You know better."

I guess I'd forgotten all the reasons for the divorce was the thought that crossed Ryan's mind.

Claire got a little tautological on women's sport clothes, and Ryan's eyes glazed over as he heard "fuchsia," "puce," and "culottes." His ears perked up at the term "tennis shorts," but he drifted off thinking of his own golfing apparel, which consisted of khaki, black, white, and blues, and other important matters. *Do I prefer ale or pilsner? Bitburger or Löwenbräu?*

"Ryan, what do you think about these fashion trends?" Claire asked.

"Yes, fashion. Important. We need it."

"You haven't been listening at all!" Claire was fuming. "That's your problem. You're a bore, a misogynist, and furthermore, you dress in drab colors."

"Don't have a hissy fit, Claire," Ryan said defensively. "I just think that pink, orange, red, and whatever are not for me. I just can't wrap my head around what you're talking about."

Lexi's eyes opened; she was a lioness on a hunt. "Claire, I know you're into women's lib—I'm sure you're reading Betty Friedan, Gloria Steinem, and so forth—but you're in your own world. Ryan may wear a blue uniform, white shirt, and gold wings, but his dress is always impeccable. And he's no bore. Those thoughts are what led you guys into trouble."

"Claire, buy Ryan a rust-colored sweater, how's that?" Kate offered. "But you're all being so petty. Look what's important, what's going on around us. Eastern Europe is bursting. People who live five miles from us in Berlin want religious freedom and freedom of speech, and they're tired of this huge discrepancy in the standard of living between East and West. It won't be long before we see Soviet tanks rolling into the Fulda Gap or a huge revolution in the East. It's a matter of time. Why don't we talk of something interesting, like Graf von Stauffenberg?"

"Graf who?" asked Claire.

"Never mind, Claire," Kate answered. "He led a revolt against Hitler in 1944. But I made my point."

"Let's cool down," Ryan said. "We should be thinking of how dangerous this confrontation is between the United States and the Soviet Union. It's draining treasuries and, well, it could lead to war. It's a tinderbox over here. And Claire, one of your problems is you know the price of everything but the value of nothing."

Tempers cooled some, but cool was the operative word. The small talk was forced, and they soon decided to leave. After dinner, they went to the *stube* for a nightcap and more small talk. After a drink, Ryan tried to think his way out of an upcoming dilemma. *What's the protocol here? Do I give Claire a peck first and then an air kiss to Kate and then say good night to them both as Lexi and I head to our room, or what? Maybe a kiss on each cheek. Who's going to think what? Just wing it,* he thought. "Great seeing you Claire. Hi to the kids if you see them first. *Guten nacht,* Kate."

There were "laters" and "another time" all around. Ryan had just a pang of regret. His words, the divorce, and being around three women tugged at him. For some reason, in his mind he played with visualizations: Claire as Dinah Shore, Lexi as Doris Day, and Kate as Natalie Wood.

CHAPTER SEVEN

Come fly with me, let's fly, let's fly away
If you can use some exotic booze
There's a bar in Bombay
Come on and fly with me, let's fly away
— Sammy Cahn/Jimmy Van Heusen

RYAN WAS SITTING IN the cockpit in Frankfurt with Bob Baker, a captain new to Berlin operations. They were waiting for the passengers to board before they started the pushback from the gate. Bob had a totally bald pate and could stand to lose at least thirty pounds. An announcement in German crackled over the air. *"Kommandozentral, Lufthansa eins null acht, drücken und freigabe, tor acht zwei."* This was a Lufthansa pilot asking for permission to push back from his gate for engine start and to get route clearance.

Ground control replied, "Lufthansa 108, you must speak in English, as you know."

Lufthansa 108 replied in English, "I am a German *capitan* in a German airplane at a German airport. Why must I speak English?"

A few seconds of silence was broken by a British accent, obviously a British Airways pilot. "Because you lost the bloody war!" The Lufthansa pilot was silent for a few seconds before he came back with the same request, this time in English.

That brought to Ryan's mind a story about Frankfurt and its short-tempered German air controllers. They expected crews to know their gate parking locations; they wouldn't offer any assistance from them. He had heard about the following exchange between Frankfurt ground control and a British Airways flight after landing.

Speedbird 108: "Top of the morning Frankfurt, Speedbird 108 clear of the active runway."

Ground: "*Guten morgen*! Cleared to taxi to your gate." The British Airways plane came to a stop. Ground asked, "Speedbird, do you not know where you are going?"

Speedbird 108: "I'm somewhat unfamiliar with the airport. Stand by. Please call my turns. My first officer is looking up our gate location now."

Ground (with some impatience): "Speedbird 108, you have never flown to Frankfurt before?"

Speedbird 108 (icily): "Yes, I have, a few times in 1944 and 1945. In another Boeing ... but I didn't bother to land."

Before Bob and Ryan got pushback clearance for their flight to Warsaw, he thought back to the previous evening. Lexi and Ryan had been sitting in their Berlin apartment on an autumn day just writing bills and handling correspondence. He asked her if she wanted to hear some airline jokes. She said, "Yes! You know I like them."

"Here are a few," he said, and started in on a story about a Clipper 747 landing very long on runway 07 right at the Frankfurt airport. "Tower said, 'Clipper 107, turn left on taxiway Foxtrot and hold short of 07 left.'

"The Clipper pilot said, 'I don't think I can make foxtrot, I'll try for taxiway Delta. But I'll hold short of 07 left.'

"The tower replied, 'If you don't make Delta, exit on the

autobahn and turn left to get to the terminal. In that case, don't worry about 07 left.'"

He went on with an exchange at O'Hare:

Tower: "Eastern 702, contact Departure on 124.7."

Eastern pilot: "Tower, Eastern 702 switching to Departure ... By the way, after we lifted off, we saw some kind of dead animal on the far end of the runway."

Tower: "Continental 635, cleared for takeoff; did you copy the report from Eastern?"

Continental pilot: "Continental 635, roger, cleared for takeoff; and affirmative, we copied Eastern and we've already notified our caterers."

The following exchange was heard on one flight: Tower: "You have traffic at ten o'clock, six miles!"

Pilot receiving the warning: "Give us another hint. We only have digital watches."

Ground Control: "Finnair 209, bear to the left, disabled aircraft on the right."

Finnair pilot: "Finnair 209 roger, I have the disabled aircraft in sight, but I do not see the bear."

The following was supposedly heard at LAX: When the crew of a US airliner made a wrong turn during taxi and came nose to nose with another aircraft, the furious female ground controller screamed: "[Call sign], where are you going? I told you to turn right on Charlie taxiway; you turned on Delta. Stop right there." She continued her harangue with "You've screwed everything up. It'll take forever to sort this out. You stay right there and don't move until I tell you to. You can expect progressive taxi instructions after I put you in the penalty box. In about a half hour I will tell you exactly where to go, when to go, and how to go. Acknowledge!"

The frequency went quiet until an unknown male pilot broke the silence and asked, "Wasn't I married to you once?"

"Did you know that our cockpits are now upgraded for automatic landings? This is really true," Ryan told Lexi. "We can actually use the autopilot to land the airplane, with auto throttles and all, just by setting a few markers on the airspeed indicator and maneuvering with the autopilot. It's wonderful for landings in zero visibility, although we're not certified for that yet. We do test it in good weather. though. It will be certified eventually. It's amazing to see the throttles actually being magically brought back just before touchdown. In the future, there'll be only a pilot and a monkey in the cockpit. The trained monkey will be there to hit the pilot if he touches anything.

Ryan didn't let Lexi off the hook with that one. "I sometimes hear a passenger asking an agent if he or she is on a nonstop flight. Isn't that ridiculous, since the plane has to stop somewhere? Also, at a gate you hear an agent say it's time to *preboard*, and then people *board*. That's a little dumb too, because *preboard* is something you do before you *board*. Finally, you'll hear a flight attendant say after landing to keep your seatbelts fastened until the airplane comes to a complete stop. What's a partial stop?

"That's it for now," he said.

"I'll wait for the next installment."

"Hey, do you want to see a movie tonight? The American movie *Dirty Dancing* with Patrick Swayze is just two blocks away—I saw a posting on a billboard. I'm sure it's in English with German subtitles."

"Sounds good. Let's go to the Hartke House for dinner, next door to the movie."

The clerk at the box office said, with a smile on his face, "You want to see this American movie?" Ryan said yes, and the clerk said something like, "Have fun." It turned out the movie was entirely dubbed in German, no subtitles. The Germans, they found out, were perfect at dubbing. Anyhow, they got the theme of this entertaining but simplistic movie without words. As they came out, the box office clerk asked, "Enjoy?"

Ryan said, "*Ja wohl, danke.*" Another lesson learned. They turned in early since they were both flying the next day.

So back to the flight at hand, Bob and Ryan were to fly from Frankfurt to Warsaw and then on to Krakow, Poland for a layover, and Lexi was aboard. They got clearance for the pushback and their traffic control clearance. Bob asked, "How about some responsive reading? Prestart checklist."

Ryan began with reading the checklist for engine start. They got the engines started and were soon on their way to Warsaw. As they were cruising to Warsaw, Bob asked him about his flying background. He told the captain he'd been a navy pilot.

"Were you a carrier pilot?" the captain asked.

"No, I was carrier qualified in two kinds of aircraft, but I flew multiengine patrol planes operationally. I'm a card-carrying member of the Tailhook Association. Antisubmarine warfare was my specialty. I chose multiengine to build up my hours for the airlines. Anyhow, how long have you been with Contrails, Bob?"

"Thirty years."

"Almost ready for retirement, huh?"

Bob seemed insulted. "Are you calling me old?"

"No sir, just doing the math."

"Well, it's not the miles you've traveled but the roads you've traveled on."

"Or the airways, as it were. What did you do in the service?"

"I was a captain in the air force. Got out before Vietnam, thank goodness. Now I'm wearing four stripes."

"No disrespect, Bob, but you know there's a big difference between an airline captain and a navy captain?"

"No. They're both respected and have a lot of responsibility."

"True, but Bob, as an airline pilot, as long as you can fly the airplane satisfactorily and pass check rides, which become routine, you'll be promoted to captain, but the when depends on a lot of variables. As long as you don't come across as Quasimodo. Now, being a military O-6, that's a navy captain, or an air force or army full colonel, you have to go through a lot of wickets to get that fourth stripe. At every promotion, a selection board compares you to all the other officers in the promotion zone. To get, let's say in the navy, from lieutenant to lieutenant commander, there's about an eighty-five percent chance of being selected. To get to the next level, a commander, you have about a seventy-five percent chance of getting selected. To get the nod from a captain's selection board, you have about a sixty percent chance. You need an advanced degree and have interservice work, and you have to have commanded a ship or a squadron. And you had to have attended a senior service college, such as a war college. I had them all. But I knew the system. I knew how to work with the detailer—the officer who assigns you to billets. But multiply those probabilities together, and to get from a lieutenant to a navy captain, your chances are about thirty-three percent, while your chance of making an airline captain is about a hundred percent. As I said, I got promoted by lobbying my detailer and having high-ranking officers lobby for me."

"That's nonsense! Why did you leave the navy in the first place?"

"It's a fact captain, although the probabilities vary from year to year, depending on guidance the Secretary of the Navy gives to the selection board. But I got out of the navy for several reasons. I didn't like the family separations, even though I didn't have that many. I didn't like the hierarchy structure, the pay wasn't that great, we got moved every three years, which meant we had no chance to build up equity in a home, and I knew that as I got promoted I wouldn't be flying airplanes, I'd be shuffling papers. I like to fly. You can't really self-actualize by flying, but it's fun. So I wrote articles, got advanced degrees, and built a family. That's why I got promoted. So why did I leave the service? I like to fly, and I like time off. I didn't like to report to seniors in the military I thought might have reached their levels of incompetence, and I like airline pay. But as you know, things are changing. I've had the wonderful good fortune of making careers of both.

"But my heart always went out to those aviators who were carrier based during the Vietnam War. Their deployments were sometimes extended to nine months. When on station, they would sometimes fly two or three flights a day around the clock for weeks on end. Depending on the type of aircraft, there could be eighteen aircrews, a pilot and a naval flight officer in each, in a squadron. Several aircraft would be launched on a mission. Often all aircraft would return to the ship, but sometimes two or even three aircraft would never return. The chances of a given aircraft not returning depended on the type of aircraft, the mission, and the phase of the war. At the peak of the war, the probability of being shot down on a given sortie and killed or captured was anywhere between one and five percent—maybe more. But probabilities were all over the board and therefore meaningless. There were so many variables in a given flight. The chances of being downed might be like flipping a coin and having it come up heads five or six straight times, or the odds could be worse. That could have been me, easily. I'm blessed beyond all belief.

"At the peak of the war, some aviators intuited that their luck had run out. It just wasn't worth it being launched into the dark on a stormy night for a mission that might involve dropping bombs on a truck barn while seeing surface-to-air missiles coming at you. Of course, part of the deal was you had to land your bird on the carrier in horrible weather while perhaps being damaged by flak. Some aviators—a fair number at times—simply turned in their wings and refused to fly. Even though that would end their careers, they may have had a service obligation remaining, which meant they'd be assigned to some mind-numbing job in God knows where and probably unaccompanied by dependents. Still, to some that was preferable to continuing to fly meaningless missions with a good chance of buying the farm. On one day in December 1972, six B-52s were shot down over North Vietnam. Thirty-six men lost—killed or captured.

"My aircraft was hit several times, but we never went down. One interesting quick story is about the time we landed in Cam Ranh Bay in South Vietnam. Its airport sits on a beautiful, crystal-blue bay. The runway was made of Marsten matting at the time, you know, that metal-grid type of runway. Easy to construct, but rough to land on. Once, somebody came running out to tell us there was a huge snake—probably a python—in his room. Another time, our crew decided to go swimming. Before we got out of the water, there were little splashes all around us—we were being shot at. Nobody got hit, but we swam fast. Gosh, I have so many memories of being in 'Nam."

The flight to Warsaw was routine. The landing, offloading, and loading were normal, and they were soon on their way for the short hop to Krakow. This city was quite historic, being the home of Copernicus and Pope John Paul II. The terminal was quite small. They cleared customs and went to their hotel. They normally stayed at Intercontinental or Hilton hotels, but in Krakow they always stayed at the Holiday Inn—apparently the best hotel in town. Their Polish flight attendants gave them a tour of the very interesting city. Lexi and Ryan bought an antique figurine that, they were told by the vendor, was not allowed to leave Poland because of historic value. Ryan later packed it in his flight bag anyhow.

Lexi and Ryan spotted Bob at a nearby table in the hotel dining room looking like he was going to dine by himself. Ryan asked him to join them, and he reluctantly agreed. He seemed like a nice enough guy but was rather taciturn. After looking over the extensive menu, Lexi ordered broiled salmon. The waiter said, "Sorry, madam, we are out of that dish."

"Okay, how about the stuffed pork chops?" Lexi countered.

"I'm sorry, madam; we are out of that dish also."

"Well, what do you have or recommend?"

"We have chicken only."

"Fine, baked chicken breasts for both of us." As Ryan recalled, Bob had the same thing.

The next morning, the three met in the lobby with the flight attendants for the ride to the airport. Lexi cleared immigration and was stamped out of Poland for the flight to Warsaw, their next stop, then on to Berlin. But a problem arose there in Warsaw. The flight was full, and the captain insisted Lexi get off the plane since she was flying on a space-available basis. Ryan said, "Bob, you know, here in our Berlin base we operate like a squadron—we get our dependents on the plane no matter what. Put her in the cockpit or in the lavatory for takeoff, and she can then ride in one of the flight attendant's jump seats. She's been booked to Berlin."

"Sorry, that's against the rules."

"Maybe in America, where you just came from, but things are different here. Come on, put her on."

"Sorry, no way," came his response. "I'm not going to get into trouble."

Ryan pondered the matter. He knew Lexi was resourceful and a world traveler; she'd just go to the crew hotel and catch the Contrails flight the next day. He knew she could handle the situation, but he wasn't happy, and the flight engineer was livid. He said, "Bob, she's already been stamped out of Poland, and you're going to leave her here behind the Iron Curtain?"

"Sorry, yes."

The station manager was in the cockpit during the passenger loading and assured them she'd take care of Lexi. Ryan found out later it was a holiday in Poland, the hotels were filled, and all train seats out of Warsaw had been reserved. The manager made some calls and got Lexi a flight with LOT, the Polish airline. Lexi was put in a seat that kept falling back, a seat that would never have been used in America. But this was Poland, and since she had to get out of the country, she sat upright on the flight to East Berlin.

She told Ryan later that for the short flight the attendants gave out only a piece of hard candy. On takeoff, the overhead bins were open with no doors, and on the roll, things fell into the aisle. She got to Schönefeld Airport in East Berlin, where

Contrails never flew, but her troubles were not over. She had to buy an S-Bahn ticket to get to West Berlin, but she had only deutschmarks, West German money, and needed reichsmarks, the East German money. Since it was Sunday, none of the places to change money was open, so she began crying. An East German policeman told her she could buy coffee with deutschmarks and get change in reichsmarks. The smallest she had was a twenty deutschmark bill, and the coffee shop gave her change on a one-for-one basis; that cup of coffee cost her well over twenty dollars, but she got her ticket and made her way to West Berlin and their apartment. Ryan was surprised to see her. She cried again as she told him her story. He realized he should have just told the captain in Warsaw he was sick and couldn't fly. The captain would have had to cancel the flight or put Lexi aboard. It was yet another learning experience.

Pilots usually reported for their flights about an hour before departure time. They read the bulletin boards, made Jeppeson (the company that provides aeronautical charts and regularly updates them) chart changes to their flight manuals, and just shot the breeze with other pilots. On his first flight after the Warsaw fiasco, Ryan spread the word about the Warsaw incident in Berlin's Contrails' operations locker room and lounge, and Bob Baker became somewhat of a pariah among the pilots. He surely got a talking-to by some of the senior captains.

Lexi's problem with getting the reichsmarks she'd needed made Ryan think of how funny money could be in Europe. He'd known station managers behind the Iron Curtain, in Warsaw, Krakow, Zagreb, Bucharest, and other cities where they laid over, who would meet them in the cockpit after the passengers disembarked and change money for them from deutschmarks or dollars for the local currency for about seven times the official exchange rate. Hard currency was highly valued in the Eastern Bloc, and the managers would make a tidy profit as they reversed the trade locally. Also, in Bucharest, the manager would always bring Beluga caviar to the cockpit to sell to them for a very low price—as long as it was in hard currency.

Speaking of station managers, the one who had helped Lexi in Warsaw was very attractive. On another flight to Warsaw, Ryan saw her in the hotel lobby in a sleek dress, very well made up. His suspicion was that she had a lucrative moonlighting job. When you live in the Eastern Bloc, any extra income helps.

CHAPTER EIGHT

I believe I can fly
I believe I can touch the sky
I think about it every night and day
Spread my wings and fly away

—R. Kelly

RYAN KNEW SOMETIMES HARD landings just happened. A sudden gust or a crosswind could alter an otherwise perfect approach, and a pilot could land with the nose misaligned with the runway. Or he could make the final flare, or pushover, for landing too soon or too late and rattle everybody's teeth. It had happened to Ryan more than once. After one less-than-perfect landing, as Ryan was saying good-bye to the passengers at the cockpit door, a little old lady asked him, "Sir, was that landing intentional or were we shot down?" After they made that landing, he overheard a flight attendant tell the folks over the PA, "Please check the overhead bins carefully as you open them, because after a landing like that, sure as heck things have been quite rearranged."

Ryan was once ferrying an empty plane to Berlin from Geneva after an engine change and made an interesting landing. Lexi was in the cockpit, and it was at night. There was nobody in back—just four of them up front. Yes, things like that happened in the German operations. Minus about 110 passengers and bags, they were about twenty-three thousand pounds lighter than normal. Ryan made a good approach and flared with no wind. He touched down nicely, and touched down nicely again, and one more time. He said aloud, "Whoa big fellow, whoa!" It was the old kangaroo hop. Even though he had adjusted his approach airspeed for a lighter weight, he just couldn't prevent the bouncing. It would have been embarrassing otherwise, but he had plenty of runway. The captain just smiled, but Ryan had to start blabbering to Lexi about the complexities of landing a plane. She also just smiled.

Takeoffs and landings were the most challenging parts of any flight for all pilots, including Ryan. Before takeoff, he'd calculate a V1 speed, the speed the aircraft could reach, lose an engine, and still stop on the runway using brakes only. Reverse thrust helped the aircraft stop even more quickly, but it was not used in the calculation; that was just a safety cushion. Reverse thrusters were just "clam shells" that opened on landing to redirect thrust forward, or, in other words, apply all the thrust to what was basically a barn door on each engine to brake thrust.

A lot of things could go wrong on takeoffs. An engine could fail near V1, and the failure of an outboard engine on a four-engine or two-engine aircraft could cause a violent swerve because of the asymmetrical thrust. If the runway was wet, stopping the plane near V1 after engine failure was much more difficult due to the hydroplaning effect, which reduced friction, making the brakes less effective, and also the aircraft would be riding on a film of water, which reduced friction further.

The causes of engine loss were varied, anything from an internal failure or foreign object damage caused by something being sucked into an engine. As an example, the crash of the Concorde in 2000 was caused by a piece of metal on the runway puncturing its tires; they burst, which punctured its fuel tanks, and the fuel was ignited by an electrical spark. The massive fire caused the loss of two engines, and the aircraft became uncontrollable.

An engine loss shortly after takeoff was serious, especially if it involved an engine fire or multiple engine loss, as could be the case with bird strikes. This called for an immediate landing, and it could be that the aircraft weighed considerably more than what it was supposed to on landing because of all the fuel it was carrying at that time. The crew may not have had time to dump fuel to reduce weight, and they wouldn't want to have the dumped fuel, which came out of nozzles near the wingtips, anywhere near an engine fire. Fuel dump was usually done over water or in the desert and was a costly procedure done only when the aircraft has to land *in extremis*. So a plane with a lot of fuel could be grossly overweight when it landed in such an emergency, and that could result in a blown tire, which had all sorts of ramifications. After such a landing, the plane would be checked out for structural integrity before the next takeoff.

If a passenger had a heart attack immediately after or soon after takeoff, the pilot was obligated to land at the nearest suitable field. If such an airport was not supported by the airline involved, the passengers could be in for a long delay after the patient was disembarked and qualified mechanics inspected the plane or a substitute aircraft was flown in.

An Air Florida flight crashed in 1982, shortly after taking off in snowy and icy conditions at National Airport in Washington, DC. The aircraft had not been deiced properly, which was the main cause of the crash. However, the pilots had been engaged in frivolous talk between engine start and takeoff. Had they paid more attention to the weather conditions, they may have been able to prevent the accident. Numerous protocols came about after that accident, and much more emphasis was placed on crew coordination and teamwork. No longer did authoritarian captains dominate cockpit culture. Airlines started insisting on a "sterile cockpit" between engine start (or shutdown in the case of an arriving aircraft) and the time a plane reached ten thousand feet (or when a plane went below ten thousand feet, coming in for a landing), leaving no room for unprofessional comments or bantering among the cockpit crewmembers below that ten-thousand-foot altitude. It had proven to be an effective tool in preventing incidents. Before the Air Florida crash, an Eastern crew was so concerned about getting a stuck landing gear down as they approached Miami International that they forgot to fly the aircraft and inadvertently landed in the Everglades. When any problem in flight occurs, a pilot's first rule was to "first fly the airplane."

Altimeter settings were crucial. A radar altimeter and a pressure altimeter were both in the cockpit. The former emitted an electronic pulse down and converted the time it took for the signal to return into distance. It was accurate, but it required electric power, so it was a backup to the pressure altimeter, just called the "altimeter," which was based on the outside air's pressure and required no electrical input. It generally displayed the aircraft's height above sea level and required a manual input of a pressure setting.

Since America really pioneered aviation in most respects, international flying used English as the official language and feet as the official measurement for altitudes. In spite of this, almost all countries otherwise used the metric system for weights and measures. Flying in Eastern Europe presented Ryan with at least three challenges. First, many controllers spoke English, but sometimes their accents were heavy. Second, the metric system used for altitude assignments required a conversion chart in the cockpit since altimeters were calibrated in feet.

Third, and perhaps most critical, was the use of pressure

altimeter settings. Most of the world reported local pressure mathematically corrected to sea level. That is, an airport would report pressure at that airport as if it were at sea level, given the surrounding air mass. Therefore, on the ground in the West, an aircraft's altimeter would show height above sea level. In the Eastern Bloc, however, stations reported actual pressure with no correction to sea level. Therefore, on the ground, an altimeter would show an altitude of zero. An international airline pilot understood this, but it introduced one more factor into the variables that could cause accidents.

At cruise altitudes anywhere in the world, above a certain altitude (eighteen thousand feet in the United States), standard sea level pressure was set into an altimeter to ensure proper vertical separation of aircraft.

Of particular concern to pilots were wind shear and microbursts. An aircraft flying through smooth, nonturbulent air doesn't know if it was flying through a headwind or a tailwind; it was simply flying through a mass of air and was moving with the air mass. Its ground speed, of course, would vary with the amount of the headwind or tailwind component. An aircraft with 200 knots of true airspeed would have a ground speed of 180 knots if it was going through a 20-knot headwind, but it would have a ground speed of 220 knots with a 20-knot tailwind. (A nautical mile is one minute of latitude, a little over a 1.1 statute mile, and a knot is one nautical mile per hour.)

Wind shear and microbursts could play havoc with an airplane. Wind shear was defined by winds that changed significantly in speed and/or direction over a short distance horizontally or vertically. A microburst was a small but intense downdraft from a thunderstorm or from another form of extremely unstable air. When the downdraft hit the ground, it would spread out with a speed that could exceed 100 knots. A violent downdraft could slam an aircraft down with disastrous results if close to the ground. With a microburst, a violent tailwind could rapidly change the true airspeed of an airplane and cause a reduction of airflow over the wings, and in extreme conditions could cause airspeed to decrease below its stall speed, again with disastrous results. A gradual but significant increase in a tailwind would not affect the plane as its inertia would adjust to the change. These phenomena could lead to accidents for a variety of reasons, including sudden crosswinds, incorrect altimeter settings because of sudden pressure changes, stalls, and violent downdrafts.

St. Elmo's Fire was a frightening phenomenon that could occur in thunderstorms. This "fire" was a mixture of gas and plasma that caused ionization of air molecules. It could appear on a pilot's windshield at night as a dancing, bright, glowing spiderweb. When a pilot first experienced the effect, it could seem as though the whole windshield was going to burst, although that didn't happen. It could, however, cause a discharge that in itself was innocuous but certainly caught the pilot's attention, especially when nerves were on edge because of heavy rain and turbulence.

Another concern was an extreme angle of bank. An aircraft's stall speed increased with its angle of bank, something Ryan and all other pilots learned in basic flight training. When a pilot would overshoot a runway on an approach, he would sometimes give in to the tendency to "wrap it up," to align with the runway, which could lead to approach-turn stalls. It was beaten into trainees' heads, but it still happened.

Ryan recalled going through flight training in the 1960s and meeting quite a few South Vietnamese pilots going through training also as the war heated up. Of course, at that time not many of them spoke or understood English that well. They probably absorbed about 75 percent of what ground school was trying to teach them, but they learned one thing well.

Instructors always pounded into them that when they lost an engine, they had to transmit, "Mayday, Mayday, Mayday!" As Ryan was strapping himself into his T-28 aircraft one day, he heard over the air, "Mayday, Mayday, Mayday!" The tower went on the air immediately with the transmission: "Aircraft calling Mayday—state your location!" A foreign voice came over the air in broken English. "I am on flight line, and my engine just quit!" Somebody had missed the concept that "Mayday" was for very serious airborne emergencies mainly.

Aviation was terribly unforgiving of carelessness, incapacity, or neglect, and this meant human error. Incapacity took many forms. Because reflexes slow with age, the Federal Aviation Administration mandated that pilots couldn't fly commercial planes beyond the age of sixty during the 1980s, but they could serve as flight engineers. Stories about pilots flying while intoxicated or "high" were numerous. Rules varied among airlines, but the general rule was eight hours between "bottle and throttle." Ryan had at times smelled alcohol on a pilot's breath in a cockpit. Most airlines had diversion programs whereby pilots with substance abuse problems could return to the cockpit after treatment. Obviously, such pilots were monitored. As well, personal problems could interfere with attention, and eyesight and nerves degenerated with age.

Which brought Ryan to a problem he seemed to be facing in a serious way: his hands were shaking more than ever. When a fellow pilot comment on it once, Ryan tried to brush it off. "Just some things going on in my life. I'm fine." Of course, an alcoholic who needed a drink could shake, but Ryan started to think about Parkinson's disease.

He had Lexi and Kate onboard for one memorable flight to Athens. Russian controllers were hard to understand, but Greek controllers were worse. They sounded like they had mush in their mouths. He was cleared while fairly near the airport to proceed direct to Thessaloniki, although it was a vague approximation of that name. If he hadn't remembered the city from history, he would have been lost. After they landed and the passengers got off, three military guards with AK-47s met the flight crew plus Kate and Lexi, walked them through customs, onto the bus, and to the hotel. The crew was told to take their hats off while on the bus for security reasons, and the route the bus took to and from the hotel always varied. They took hijacking and terrorism very seriously in Athens.

Ryan, Lexi, and Kate took a cab to the base of the Acropolis and made the climb to the Parthenon. Ryan really felt awe in his heart and mind, being there with two lovely women and in a place where so much history had transpired.

That night they enjoyed a couple of ouzo drinks before dinner and dined on moussaka, dolmades, and lamb kabobs. Of course the Greeks made fine wine, and they enjoyed that as well.

Chapter Nine

Gonna break these chains around me
Gonna learn to fly again
May be hard, may be hard
But I'll do it

—Diane Warren

THE 1980S WERE TRANSFORMATIVE. The Soviet Bloc experienced unrest, particularly in East Berlin and East Germany. Ronald Reagan became president in 1981, and Mikhail Gorbachev became the general secretary of the Soviet Union's Communist Party in 1985, when the country was deeply involved in Afghanistan. In 1986, America's *Challenger* space shuttle blew up shortly after liftoff. Soon, a devastating explosion occurred at the Soviet nuclear power plant in Chernobyl in the Ukraine, which alarmed the world. Nevertheless, the two leaders met several times in the 1980s and discussed issues of great importance, agreeing on some issues and disagreeing on others. They met in Iceland, Washington, DC, and in Europe. They were both men of great patriotic pride but grew to trust, respect, and even like each other. Gorbachev knew his country could not hope to match America in defense spending and still keep some semblance of a decent lifestyle for its citizens. Gorbachev instituted *glasnost*, openness, and *perestroika*, restructuring, in his country. The two leaders were affable, open-minded, and pragmatic. In the meantime, there was great unrest in all of Eastern Europe. On June 12, 1987, at the steps of Berlin's historic Brandenburg Gate, President Reagan gave his famous speech. "General Secretary Gorbachev, if you seek peace—if you seek prosperity for the Soviet Union and Eastern Europe—if you seek liberalization: come here, to this gate. Mr. Gorbachev, open this gate. Mr. Gorbachev, tear down this wall."

It is generally agreed this speech was the beginning of the end of the Cold War. Ryan knew he was living in a period of great historical significance. The first stirrings of change in Eastern Europe came in Poland in 1989, when the government and Lech Walesa, the leader of the opposition, agreed in April to free elections for the country's national assembly. Two months later, the communists lost all but one contested seat. In the same month in Prague, some ten thousand East Germans sought asylum at the West German embassy, climbing over its gates and pitching tents on the grounds. In September, some sixty thousand more East Germans fled to Hungary. Hungary soon announced that any Germans in Hungary would be allowed to enter Austria, and tens of thousands of East Germans went to Hungary. On November 9, 1989, an East German spokesman announced that the GDR had decided to issue travel visas to any citizen who wanted to leave the country. That evening, masses pushed through Berlin's checkpoint at Bornholmer Strasse, and by midnight, all of the checkpoints along the Wall were opened. The world witnessed an event of great historic importance.

Lexi and Ryan had returned to Berlin from a flight on the evening of November 9. They heard that masses were gathering at the Wall, not knowing it would come down late that night. He and Lexi went to the Wall the next day with a hammer and took some small chunks of the rubble. November 10 was chaotic in West Berlin as East Berliners crowded the streets to see what they had been missing all those years and to reunite with relatives and friends. The banks were jammed also, as West Germany gave bonuses, called "freedom money" to "refugees" from the East, 100 deutschmarks each. East Germans rode a subway for the first time and saw wonderful department stores where clerks actually gave a damn. "Ode to Joy" by Beethoven was heard everywhere for several days.

November 9 was a significant day in Berlin's history for several reasons. It was the anniversary of Hitler's *putsch* in Munich in 1923, the anniversary of an attempt on Hitler's life in Munich in 1939, and the anniversary of *Kristallnacht* in 1938, a time when Jewish-owned stores, buildings, and synagogues were vandalized; broken glass covered the streets of the city on that sinister day.

Ryan's problem was getting worse. He'd always been an athlete. He was six foot two and weighted about 215. He'd always participated in sports and had run marathons, even at his weight, because his body fat was low. As he did more research into Parkinson's, he noticed more tremors in the right side of his body as well as involuntary movements in his fingers and arm, and Lexi noticed his posture wasn't normal. His balance would occasionally get out of kilter, and he experienced some dizziness now and then. He also had some problems buttoning his shirt and brushing his teeth. His research led him to believe he had the disease, perhaps stage one. He could still function but wasn't sure how long he could get away with it or hide it. He'd passed his last flight physical in October 1989 but had to do some slow, careful printing on the paperwork. The German company doctor was congenial and was more interested in conversing than examining. Ryan had two beers before the exam to calm his nerves and told the doctor he wasn't able to give a urine sample—just didn't have to go. He didn't want him to find any alcohol in his system. The doctor was fine with that and passed him.

It was the Christmas season, a magical time in Germany in general and Berlin in particular. All the major cities had downtown vendors selling ornaments and other season specialties. Munich and Nuremberg had especially nice markets. Snow covered the ground, and the temperature hung at freezing or below. Ryan and Lexi enjoyed having Pam, Ryan's daughter, join them for about ten days over the holidays. They took her to Istanbul before Christmas, and she and Lexi stayed a couple of days in Switzerland to see the sights. They had Christmas Eve dinner at the famous Kempinski Hotel in Berlin. Todd was in college and opted to spend the holidays in San Diego with friends. At night they would walk downtown Berlin, buy marzipan and hot chocolate at a confectionary store, and get a sense of how much the Germans loved Christmas. Ryan had trouble writing Christmas cards, so he did a lot of printing. Germans celebrated New Year's by shooting handguns and fireworks into the air atop apartment buildings.

Lexi and Ryan sat in their apartment one evening in January 1990, drinking mulled wine and talking about an upcoming trip to California for his recurrent training in San Francisco and spending a few days at their San Diego home. He got around to telling her some more airline stories.

"Lexi, at the end of a flight, the engineer writes up discrepancies or 'squawks' or 'gripes' that maintenance must fix, if they are safety issues, before the next flight. Well, I wrote down some problems and solutions I've heard of. Here's the paper:"

Problem: Left inside main tire almost needs replacement.

Solution: Almost replaced the left inside main tire.

Problem: Test flight okay, but auto-land very rough.

Solution: Auto-land not installed on this aircraft.

Problem: Something loose in cockpit.

Solution: Something tightened in cockpit.

Problem: Evidence of leak on right main landing gear.

Solution: Evidence removed.

Problem: Autopilot in altitude-hold mode produces a 200 foot-per-minute descent.

Solution: Could not duplicate on ground.

Problem: Number-three engine missing occasionally.

Solution: Number-three engine found on right wing and seems to stay there.

Problem: Dead bugs on windshield.

Solution: Dead bugs removed; live ones on back order.

"I could go on. Things like these happened more in the navy that in the airlines."

"You know, to get serious now," Lexi said, "I fear that with your condition, our days in Berlin with Contrails may be numbered. I'm very worried. Your health is our first priority.

But we're okay financially. Thank goodness you have loss-of-license insurance and military retirement pay, and we sure have a lot of great memories."

"I wouldn't trade our time here for anything. I remember not only the adventures but also the little things. Remember when we'd fly to Frankfurt or Stockholm just to visit old friends? Or take a train to Prague for a couple of days? Recall when we flew as passengers that after takeoff virtually everyone onboard would light up a cigarette and the cabin turned blue? The Germans loved to smoke, and many guys still smoke in the cockpit."

"I loved Prague," Lexi said. "The castle, the royal museum, the bridges across the Vltava, Wenceslas Square, the great restaurants, and the twelfth- and thirteenth-century buildings."

"I have good memories of all the cities. I suppose Paris is my favorite. It has to be the greatest walking-around city in the world."

"We'll miss it. But we love California. San Diego, San Francisco, Monterey, and Big Sur. Can't beat them."

CHAPTER TEN

Try to remember the kind of September
When life was slow and oh, so mellow
Try to remember the kind of September
When grass was green and grain was yellow.

—Tom Jones

LEXI AND RYAN RETURNED to California for his annual training in San Francisco in late January 1990. It involved a few days of lectures and some written exams for training purposes only—they were self-corrected. He had two days in a flight simulator to practice emergencies and instrument approaches in poor weather conditions.

The amazing flight simulators were cockpit replicas in every way; they were physically moved by hydraulic systems that provided movement in three dimensions, on all three axes. Pilots could feel roll, pitch, and yaw as well as simulated turbulence. The instructor sat behind the captain's seat with his own special instrument panel that enabled him to create various abnormal conditions and emergencies—even compound emergencies. The cockpit windows were dark until the instructor realistically varied the display through the windows to depict actual airports pilots flew to. The instructor could adjust the weather and change the airport, runways, and visibility; the whole thing seemed realistic. Ryan passed the simulator check, but he had trouble with nonprecision approaches in that he struggled to find the runway environment in poor visibility whereas his partnered captain could pick it up right away at minimums. The instructor had to run him through these approaches several times before he could perform them to the instructor's satisfaction.

"Ryan, how's your vision?" the instructor asked. "Have you had it checked recently?" Ryan said he hadn't but would do so straightaway. He had always had 20/10 vision, but he began to realize the ravages of aging were catching up to him. He made an appointment with an optometrist, who fitted him with progressive trifocals. He needed to see approach plates or charts at about twelve inches, the instrument panel at close to three feet, and the runway, which for the purpose of glasses, was at infinity.

While they were in San Francisco, Lexi and Ryan stayed at the Marines' Memorial Hotel. He had a few days off after training. He called his old friend and former flight surgeon, Vince, who lived in Tiburon. They chatted for a while and agreed to meet for dinner at Scoma's on Fisherman's Wharf. It was wonderful to see Vince and his lovely wife; they were great people and dear friends. They talked of good times in their old squadron. The ladies had lobster thermidor while Vince enjoyed halibut and Ryan had delicious salmon, an addiction of his since his days of salmon fishing in Kodiak, Alaska, when he was in the navy.

Ryan finally got around to bringing up Parkinson's. "Vince, I know you have an obligation to report people who are threats to public safety to the appropriate authority. I passed my last flight physical and cleared my check ride in the simulator this month." He explained his symptoms and concerns.

"Well of course this is just between us," Vince said. "You're not my patient, and I'm not treating you. But from what you say, I'd say you may very well have Parkinson's, in an early stage. It's treatable, but you probably know it's progressive. I frankly suggest you see a neurologist—I can refer you. But you should accept the fact that if that's the diagnosis, your flying career will soon be over. I'm sorry to tell you that, but you're still fairly young with a lot of qualifications—degrees, leadership experience, and so on. You have your military retirement, free health care, and probably a retirement from Contrails."

"I do accept it. It's been a good run, and thanks for the advice. Let's change the subject, shall we?" They talked some more and promised to meet more often.

Ryan saw a neurologist during his few vacation days after his training. He was, as he had expected, diagnosed with Parkinson's. The doctor had first asked him for a sample of his handwriting. The doctor told him it was an idiopathic disease, one with no known cause and diagnosed only by symptoms. CAT scans and MRIs could be used for confirmation but mainly to rule out other problems. The disease, Ryan learned, was believed to be caused by insufficient formation and activity of dopamine produced in certain neurons in the brain

"Ryan, although there is treatment, you're on the very edge of not being able to fly anymore," the neurologist said. "You're probably between stages one and two of the disease. I'll treat you with medication, but your condition will only progress."

"How so, doctor?"

"You're fairly young, so it may be slow to develop further. It varies in people. Later, you might see disorders of speech, cognition, mood, behavior, and thought—maybe dementia. The best things you can do now include good diet and exercise. Coffee seems to help. And, counterintuitively, so does tobacco. It's a dopamine thing, but I don't recommend you start smoking. Stay active. Keep your mind busy—reading, puzzles, and so forth. Work on your posture. Later, we can get you into physical therapy. The disease itself isn't fatal, but what later develops can be. We're all going to die of something, but don't worry unnecessarily. Except flying is probably going to be out soon."

"Doc, do me one favor," Ryan asked. "You say I'm on the edge. I passed my last flight physical. Let me fly for a couple more weeks, and I promise I'll go to the company and turn myself in. I have unfinished business in Berlin. I'll tell you when I can't fly."

"I'll do that for you, Ryan. I think you're good to go as far as flying is concerned, but just for a while. Good luck to you, but if you ever feel you can't fly, call in sick."

"I will, and thanks for your forbearance. The future is not so grim. I'll miss flying, but I don't think I'll die soon. I have to live to see my grandkids do well in life."

"You have a good attitude. You're a winner. No wonder Vince said nice words about you."

Ryan thought back to the panorama of his flight career and how lucky he'd been. He had a good friend, a helicopter pilot who had visited Claire and him in Japan during Ryan's first tour in the navy and shortly before his friend had to return to duty off North Vietnam. He told them his type of helicopter had so much armor the payload was almost nil. He was due to leave the navy in a month, had a job lined up with United Airlines, and his wife was eight months pregnant.

One day in Saigon, Ryan was lying on his bed, sipping a San Miguel beer and reading *Stars and Stripes*—the military newspaper. When he came to the "Killed in Action" section, he saw his friend's name. He first thought it was somebody else with the same name, but when Ryan's mail was delivered by a squadron buddy, it included a letter from his friend's wife informing him of the death of her husband. His friend had been shot down while trying to rescue a downed pilot in North Vietnam.

After Ryan received his wings in 1964, he completed survival training and a checkout in fleet aircraft in San Diego. The survival training was called SERE, Survival, Evasion, Resistance, and Escape, a two-week course with ground school the first week. He learned what was edible and what was not in the way of flora and fauna. He recalled that polar bear liver was toxic but couldn't imagine he'd ever be faced with that situation. He also learned how to evade capture if downed, how to behave, and what to expect in a prison camp. The second week was also a navigational test. They had no food for the first four days except for one drop by helicopter of canned foodstuffs for their group of thirty or so. At their planned destination, they were all of course captured by the instructors, who played the role of Asian enemies, basically North Vietnamese or Viet Cong at that time. They were taken to a prison compound, fed nothing but fish heads and rice, and loud discordant oriental music blared over loudspeakers constantly. They were squeezed tightly into small black boxes with the lids closed for about twenty minutes. They were put individually into soundproof rooms with no lights for a couple of hours. Then came interrogation. Instructors would slap them around with an open palm to get them to talk. They were allowed to give only their names, ranks, and serial numbers. It got pretty physical, but of course the instructors were not allowed to actually wound them. One officer and one enlisted man in their group broke because of the pressure; their careers were essentially over. Ryan had one friend who was audacious enough to smuggle wire cutters into the camp in a cutaway flight boot. He tried to snip his way out one night, was discovered, and got a freezing hosing at two in the morning in the nude. Ryan figured the guy could probably withstand the real thing.

Ryan's entire naval aviation training, from the start of preflight in Pensacola until that point, had taken almost eighteen months. During that time and indeed throughout his career, he often thought of many fatalities that had hit close to home. What would happen if you slammed into the water or the ground at two hundred miles per hour? Would your mind actually have any realization of death, or would it experience agonizing pain?

With that final training hurdle out of the way, Claire and Ryan had driven to their new three-year duty station on Whidbey Island, Washington, where they planned to stay with a navy couple for a couple of days until they found a place to rent. The husband and Ryan had gone through flight training together. During the drive up, Ryan and Claire spent a night in Roseburg, Oregon. They heard on the radio the next morning that a navy plane had crashed into a mountain in Alaska. Ryan's heart sank, for his friend was on temporary duty in Alaska. He called the duty office of his friend's squadron to find out if he had been on that airplane; he got no information over the phone but was told to stop by the office when he got there. He did so, and they gave him the bad news. They drove to the widow's apartment to give her comfort. Her parents were already there. They spent some time with her and did the best they could. They stayed in a hotel for a couple of days and spent time with her each day. They finally took over her lease and bought some of her furniture. They stayed close friends over the years to come.

Another friend from flight training had been killed

shortly after being catapulted off an aircraft carrier on his last qualification flight aboard a carrier in an F-4 aircraft. Apparently, so the story went, in his excitement he made a victory roll right into the water.

Ryan had lost these two close friends before he had even started operational flying, and he lost a third close friend in that helicopter shoot-down over North Vietnam. And of course he'd lost Rick in the car crash during flight training. And after he left his first squadron to join Contrails, his entire flight crew, with a new plane commander, ran into a mountain in Canada on a flight from Kodiak to Whidbey Island. Apparently, there was heavy icing, very strong winds, and little navigational equipment available. The plane wasn't found for over a decade. He'd flown with most of those crewmembers during his last deployment and had known them well.

When Claire and Ryan lived in the Philippines for five months, they shared a home with another navy family in an American compound in the heart of the dirt-poor city of Cavite, near Sangley Point Naval Air Station. The wife was a former Mouseketeer from the old TV show *The Mickey Mouse Club*, and the husband, a nice guy with whom they got along well, was a naval flight officer, an NFO. These aviators served as tactical coordinators, bombardier/navigators, or weapons systems officers. Later, when Ryan was at the Pentagon, he learned his friend had been serving in the right seat of an S-3, an airplane designed to be flown by two pilots. He had been in a test program to mitigate the massive loss of pilots to the airlines. These right-seat NFOs handled navigation and communications. The details were murky, but Ryan was informed his friend had been killed in an S-3 accident. Another loss.

Furthermore, when he reported to the Pentagon, he had a two-week turnover with an officer, a pilot he was to replace. After Ryan had gotten to know the man fairly well, the departing officer returned to a flying billet. After Ryan had settled into his job for a week, a clerk came running into his office to tell him the officer he'd replaced had been killed in a post-maintenance test flight. The accident was in a two-engine aircraft, and both engines had been replaced before the flight. One engine seized up, and the other propeller went into overspeed and had detached. The pilots put the plane down in a field, but it was a terrible crash. His friend survived for a little while but died en route to the hospital. Yet another loss. As it turned out, his flight coverage on his small life insurance policy had not been renewed. He either didn't have time to renew it or had just forgotten. A phone call to the insurance company by a senior Pentagon official convinced the insurance company that he had been pressed into flying service before he and his wife had really settled into their new home. The company paid his insurance.

Ryan's flashbacks took him to yet another story. About the same time he reported to the Pentagon, he heard a friend of his had taken his wife and a foreign exchange student on a trip from Virginia to Hilton Head. They departed on a short grass strip in an aero club rental airplane on a very hot and humid day, which made the density altitude high, which in turn slows the rate of climb. They were probably very overloaded with luggage, and the weight and balance was undoubtedly not done properly. They never cleared the trees at the end of the runway, and all three had been killed. It was a dumb, dumb accident by a good pilot, as Ryan recalled. Pure carelessness.

The list of such fatalities that hit so close to home was endless. Ryan knew he had indeed been fortunate.

In late January 1990, after he'd completed the recurrent training in San Francisco, Ryan made his final trip to Berlin. His first pattern took him from Frankfurt to Budapest to Bucharest, Romania, for an overnight. He had known Kate would be on the flight. Lexi was onboard and was moved to first class, and she chatted with Kate and made a commitment for dinner. The flight to Bucharest was a little over an hour. On the crew bus, Ryan marveled at the city, deep in the heart of the Eastern Bloc. It had suffered greatly during World War II, when the oil fields at nearby Ploisti were bombed. The city had an eclectic architectural feel of baroque, rococo, and neo-classic. The buses in the city were supposedly powered by butane. Driving through the city at night, they saw many restaurants and homes powered by dim sixty-watt bulbs. The country was governed by the dictatorial communist leader Nicolae Ceausescu, who was later executed with his wife in the purges that followed Eastern Europe's movements to democracy.

The crew checked into a nice InterContinetal, and Lexi and Kate made dinner plans for the hotel dining room on the third floor that offered gypsy dancing, good music, and great food. But Ryan had an errand he had to run first; he knew from previous trips to Bucharest that the first thing you did there after you got your room was to go to a money exchange on the seventh floor of the hotel. He found, just as he had on previous trips, the floor had nothing but video games and about two dozen black people, "foreign students" from Africa. All Ryan had to do was to nod at one, who would follow him into the bathroom to exchange money. Ryan thought he had done a lot of weird things in his life, but being a stranger in a strange land and following an African—probably a Muslim—into a bathroom for an unknown encounter had to be near the top. The person who followed him was a Joe Frazier—the heavyweight boxer—look-alike. He spoke English, to some degree.

Ryan said, "Change money."

"How much?"

"How about twenty dollars American?'

"Okay, mon. Give me the money, I give you some leu for ten times official."

Ryan changed money and got the hell out of there. He met Lexi and Kate at the third floor restaurant. Ryan looked at the two and, as he had done in the past, thought they were twins in many ways except for hair color. The women were anticipating a wonderful meal and an entertaining gypsy dancing show, and they appeared to be getting along well. "Sorry I'm late, but I had business to take care of," he said.

"You changed money," Kate said. "That's probably illegal. You're at risk."

"Are you kidding? In this economy, anything goes. The hotel probably gets a cut of this business anyhow."

The show, food, and wine were excellent—all for less than twenty bucks American for the three. Ryan said, "We have some serious things to talk about. I think I'll be losing my medical license and will fly no more. Berlin is changing, Germany will unite, and the capital will be moved from Bonn to Berlin. The Contrails operations in Berlin will be over. We'll all go back to the States and start anew."

"You'll go to San Francisco and be a high-powered exec in the company," Lexi said to Kate.

"And hopefully we'll stay close friends, all of us, right?" Kate asked.

"You and Ryan have a special relationship," Lexi said. "I wasn't always there in Berlin when Ryan started to have his physical problems. I think you two helped each other with your impairments. Kate, you were there. He told me what went on—he doesn't lie. I know Ryan thinks the world of you. You were there when I wasn't at times—you comforted him. Ryan is the finest person I've ever known. But you rank right up there. I know you'll always be in his heart. You're a special person, Kate, and I'm not jealous of you. Perhaps I should—many women would be. But our circumstances are unique. We're in foreign lands. Many of our usual friends are nowhere near. We've become kind of a team. We all care for each other very much. You're a friend in the finest sense. You're genuine and iconic."

"Lexi, you go too far," Kate replied. "But I'll be leaving Contrails and will be living in Atherton or somewhere on the peninsula—maybe in Hillsborough, near the airport. My future is open except for the job. I never want to lose contact with you. You're always welcome at our family home in Atherton, but I'll probably have a condo in the area."

I'll have a snowball's chance in hell of ever being in that condo, Ryan thought.

"I know Ryan," Lexi said. "His feelings for you are powerful—I accept that. I understand life and the human condition. I hope we'll always stay in touch. We'll meet at Stanford homecoming football games and have dinners together when we're in San Francisco."

"This is too emotional for me," said Ryan, wanting to excuse himself for a comfort break, but he stuck it out.

"I never want to be a wedge between you two," Kate told Lexi. "I can tell Ryan's conflicted. He loves you deeply—he can never give you up. Surely you know we have feelings for each other that have put him in a precarious position, but you must know we've never been intimate."

Lexi answered, "Ryan has already told me that, and I also appreciate your honesty. If I didn't trust our relationship, we couldn't be friends.

"Yes. I cherish you both as friends and hope we stay in touch. Let me know how he's doing, and there'll be no promise or hope for anything more."

"Fair enough," Lexi said.

"I'm so glad Ryan introduced us, Lexi. Ryan is so honorable and never did anything to lead me on, but I could see myself falling for someone like him. After meeting you and seeing the relationship the two of you have, I gained even more respect for Ryan. I realized I wanted to find someone who would be as totally committed to me as he is to you."

"You two are too serious! It's a great floor show," Ryan said, embarrassed by all the accolades.

"When we're in the San Francisco area," Lexi told Kate, "we'll definitely make plans to see you. We can see you at Stanford this fall."

Ryan left Contrails unceremoniously, retired, and their goods were shipped to San Diego. He began seeing new doctors in San Diego and started treatment for Parkinson's. He and Lexi decided they needed a break from the hectic pace of flying and all the emotional happenings over various issues, so they booked a two-week cruise to Hawaii. They visited four of the islands and relaxed, swam, read, and enjoying fine food when they weren't engaged in shipboard life, where something was always going on. He played bridge at one o'clock every afternoon, enjoyed happy hour at four o'clock, and took in floor shows every evening, a nice transition into a new life. They planned to move out of their San Diego condo to a bigger home—all on one story so they could age in place.

The Stanford homecoming game was scheduled for a Saturday in October 1990. Lexi and Kate agreed to meet for dinner at The Shadows in San Francisco the night before the game. There were smiles and kisses all around. In Lexi's eyes, Kate looked younger and more vibrant. Ryan thought her having been a flight attendant and all the travel had taken a toll on her, but she was into the career she'd wanted. Lexi told her she looked wonderful, and Kate returned the compliment to both of them, which was a lie to Ryan; he knew he was sliding the wrong way, but Lexi gave her thanks for the compliment. They engaged in small talk at the table, and Kate announced she was dating a guy she really cared for. "Jason's a lawyer who works in my dad's department, and you'd like him."

"He's a lawyer?" Ryan asked. "Good luck with that. I mean that in the best way. Law's an honorable profession, but gosh, I hope he's right for you, Kate. You deserve the best. I hope it works out."

"I sure as *hell* hope he's the right guy," Lexi added.

Kate chuckled. "You're funny, Lexi. I know you want the best for me."

"Of course I do. You know how women are. But I absolutely wish you the very best. We've become close, the three of us, and we'll always be friends."

Questions of the heart can drive you crazy, Ryan thought. *I was reaching for a dream when all I could want I had. But the capacity for love is boundless—it can't be confined.* He spoke up. "Lexi, thank you for understanding and accepting the fact that Kate was more than a friend but not a lover. When fate presents you with a treasure, you don't discard it. It's very sad when a friend you know becomes a friend you *knew*. Kate, thanks for knowing me as the man I really am and for keeping me on the straight and narrow, so to speak." As they raised their glasses in a toast, *Casablanca* flashed through his mind. "Here's looking at you kid. *Auf Wiedersehen,* Ilsa … Kate. *Gross Gott.*" He choked up.

Kate said she wouldn't miss flying. "Ryan I want you to remember the words of John Dryden: 'I'm sore wounded, but I am not slain. I'll lay me down to bleed awhile, then I'll rise to fight again.' How are you doing, Ryan? How do you *really* feel?"

"Not bad, Kate." *An angel on my left and a goddess on my right. I'll always hold dear the memory of a forbidden love.* "But you know," as his eyes continued to glisten, "two women to cherish, in different ways, forever. And that, not just this disease, is also going to hurt for a long, long time." Three sets of eyes were welling with tears.

CHAPTER ELEVEN

Eternal Father, lend thy grace
To those with wings who fly thro' space.
Thro wind and storm, thro' sun and rain,
Oh bring them safely home again.
                    —Reverend William Whiting

A YEAR HAD PASSED since Lexi and Ryan had had that dinner at The Shadows with Kate. They drove to the Stanford homecoming in October 1991. As they had lunch at Andersen's in Buellton, near Santa Barbara, on the way to Palo Alto, he said, "We haven't been to the City for some time now. It's strange we haven't heard from Katrina … I mean Katarina, or Kate. We'd promised we'd get together. Her last name was Miller or Muller. No, Mueller. I think I sent her a holiday card last year but don't remember receiving one."

"Who? Who's Katarina? Or Kate?"

"You remember, our friend from Contrails. We were all good friends. We'd go out to dinner together on layovers. Sometimes she and I would dine when you were in Virginia with your sister."

"Ryan, my sister passed a year before we went to Berlin. You and I were never apart in Berlin, except for your orientation checkout. And maybe once or twice for a day, when I was stranded somewhere. There was no Kate. I have our address book here in my purse. There's nobody by that name in our book."

"But there was. We were close, I mean in a platonic sense. We had a lot in common. She even went to Stanford."

"Ryan, now listen. You know you're sick, but we work out at the gym all the time, and you read and do puzzles—you're okay. But somehow you've created an image of a woman. Maybe you're having a little trouble with the aging process. Maybe there's something organic, or perhaps you're trying to visualize a younger me. It can happen as we get older, because we hold on to vitality or want it back. You told me you dated a little at university before Claire transferred to the Bay Area. Was there a flight attendant who reminded you of someone at school?"

"No. I never dated seriously at college. Claire and I were going to be engaged after she moved to Northern California. I don't know—it all seemed so real."

"Well, there are reasons for such things, defense mechanisms, sublimation, transference, ideation, and so forth. I don't know all the terms. We can create these fantasies. Maybe this is some form of a midlife crisis. But we can see a doctor again and sort things out. What do you remember about Berlin?"

"It's kind of a blur. I remember certain good landings, some not so good. Pilots remember these things. I know we enjoyed living there. We liked certain layovers, like Paris, Oslo, and Dubrovnik. I remember the nice Polish flight attendants. I think I remember Beata and Petra showing us around Krakow. And I remember Kate from America. I recall that you, Kate, and I were on the Acropolis."

"There was no Kate, Ryan. You and I were atop the Acropolis, just the two of us. It was a very emotional moment. I know you didn't have an affair. You're far too honorable and loyal for such a thing. We're too close and too much in love."

Ryan began to develop some vague understanding and the serenity to accept that which he couldn't change. He started to realize that as he wandered in and out of lucidity or reality or whatever funk he was in. However, he knew this with certainty—Lexi was his soul mate, and nobody could replace her. He also knew he was a warrior, strong in many ways. He'd been through everything—combat, divorce, family sickness, major injuries to himself, climbing the route to success in the military, graduate degrees and flying experimental aircraft, interservice work, Pentagon work in high-pressure situations, on and on. He knew he'd done all he could have done, and he knew he was married to a woman who was unequalled.

What does all this mean? Was Katarina a dream or a series of dreams? Was she a fantasy I created by a need to relive my flying career with the underpinnings of a pseudo-affair? Or was it real? Perhaps my mind is deteriorating due to the ravages of the disease. Am I indeed going mad? If that's the case, it's a pleasant form of psychosis that combines reality with nobility and fidelity. It follows that an unfulfilled, imaginary affection simply underscores my devotion to Lexi.

I may be sick, but I'll fight. I do math problems on the treadmill. I can multiply numbers in my mind as I exercise. Can't I? I won't give up. This subject is too touchy to bring up again. I'll just embrace the words of Robert Browning: "Grow old along with me! The best is yet to be."

AFTERWORD

EXPERIENCED PILOTS—THOSE WITH, SAY, more than a couple of thousand hours in the cockpit—constitute a special segment of society. Oh, they fall in the normal population distribution as far as intelligence, needs, personality, or neuroses are concerned. They are not Sky Gods. But they are different in subtle ways. Most folks may not notice these quirks, but they are there.

When a pilot sees contrails, his eyes may linger a moment longer than most. *What is that airplane's altitude? What type of aircraft is it? I was there once!* When someone says "Three O'clock," you may see a pilot look to his right. Those "smile" lines on either side of the eyes may not be the result of aging, but of squinting at too many sunsets. The experienced pilot knows what kind of sunglasses to wear—aviator type, probably polarized.

Seasoned pilots will always recall the pungent smell of aviation gasoline or jet fuel—that sense lingers forever. They remember landings that were squeakers, or those where the plane was just planted on the concrete. Pride has a way of keeping those thoughts alive.

Perhaps the attribute that most non-pilots would not notice

is the ingrained sense of situational awareness. The aviator is generally aware of traffic, unusual noises, or aberrations of any kind. He has an acute scan pattern of the environment and gauges of any kind in a vehicle. Their reaction times are invariably keener than average. The have experienced harrowing times that few have.

Long-time pilots may or may not attend air shows; sometimes there is a sense that "I've been there—I've done that." Others may take friends or family to these events and say, "Enjoy this—this is what the defense of America entails. Those that perform these maneuvers have immense training and nerves of steel."

It takes few triggers for a weathered pilot to sense a feeling of nostalgia. *I have traveled far and experienced much.* Some may know the almost always clear skies of Miami International Airport. Others know the often "tule" fogbound approach to Travis Air Force Base. Many recall how some sort of delay may put one into the penalty box at Heathrow. Naval aviators know that they must try to catch the number three wire on an aircraft carrier or otherwise be graded adversely.

There are those who have flown the challenging approaches to St. Thomas, Kodiak Island, Kai Tak, or other places imprinted in their memories. Some recall the spiraling approaches into a war zone, and there are those helicopter pilots who put their lives on the line picking up survivors or wounded in combat areas knowing that their chances of lifting off safely may be less than fifty per cent. Some know the "circus" that is JFK International Airport in a snowstorm. There are those who have known the glorious taste of a German beer at a layover in Frankfurt or a cold one in the oppressive heat of Guam. Others have a favorite bistro on the left bank of the Seine.

Those that flew propeller planes such as the P-2 or the DC-6 across the Pacific will recall the terms "Howgozit" or

"Point of No Return." Of course, pilots talk with their hands when describing aerobatic maneuvers. And all veteran aviators know such acronyms such as, to mention a few, APU (auxiliary power unit), RVR (runway visual range), EPR (engine pressure ratio), EGT (exhaust gas temperature), CAVU (ceiling and visibility unlimited), VMC (visual meteorological conditions), and WOXOF (ceiling and visibility zero due to fog).

Indeed, old-time pilots, or the "Band of Brothers," if you will, sometimes have reunions where war stories are told and retold. Virtually all ex-military pilots have known at least one buddy who "bought the farm"—met a tragic end. Many retired airline pilots have known at least one marriage which was dissolved because of a relationship between a cockpit crewmember and a flight attendant—at least in the "old days."

Fighter pilots know the term "Kick the tires and light the fire." Most of those pilots have enjoyed the fighter pilot breakfast of a donut, a cup of coffee, and a cigarette. Most experienced pilots have picked their ways through cumulonimbus clouds, with or without the air of radar. Some veterans recall the days of navigating with loran, sextants, consolan, and drift meters. Indeed, many flyers have known the majesty of the Alps or the Sierra Nevada from 31,000 feet and the vast whiteness that is Greenland. All pilots use the words "over" and "out," but *never* together in one response.

There will come a day when a pilot will put his wings in a display case on the wall of his den, perhaps with a few model airplanes nearby. Even though age, ennui, or a medical malady will eventually ground all aviators, these warriors will have seen much of the world and experienced things that few have. But most will have gratitude for the character building that flying provided and will reflect on a life well lived. At the end of life when the veteran pilot makes that final touchdown—hopefully a squeaker—and touches the face of God, there is one concept that will never make sense to him—complacency.

A NOTE FROM THE AUTHOR

A THEME IN THIS book has been infatuation or, by inference, the temptations of infidelity. This begs the question: when is a deep, personal relationship between two people of the opposite sex appropriate when hormones are not coursing through the body? A lawyer probably would say, "It depends." A psychologist might say, "How do you feel about that situation?" A family counselor would say, "Never!" A philosopher may say, "Whenever it is right." A poet may say, "As it would be." A pragmatist would say, "How real is real?" The many variables attached to a marriage make a question such as this able to be answered only by an individual. It is a question to be pondered. My take on this subject can be gleaned from this book. The theme of a relationship between two people of the opposite sex and outside of the realm of marriage is introduced for the reasons just mentioned.

I have never been divorced. My marriage is rock-solid—a renewal of vows after a fifty-year anniversary underscores this. However, I've witnessed enough imbroglios of this kind in my flying career that the subject had to be introduced for realism as well as interest. When Pan Am flew around the world trips without changing crews, it was called the golden age of airline flying. Perhaps, ironically, this was because few pilots ever saw the adjective "golden" attached to their wedding anniversaries.

ACKNOWLEDGMENTS

THIS BOOK WOULD NOT exist without the encouragement of my wife, who wanted me to chronicle some of the important events in our lives together. I'm grateful that my children, David Siren, JD, and Jill Meoni, MD, edited the initial drafts of this work. They observed many of the events in this story and offered helpful suggestions. I owe much to Stephen Olson, JD, a prominent attorney, my cousin and lifelong friend. His insightful and invaluable comments helped me edit the drafts. Doug Denton, another longtime and close friend and fellow navy pilot, offered valuable memories of events we shared in the navy. I was fortunate to serve as his copilot for a year, and he, being several years senior to me, taught me to be a much better pilot and officer. He was my mentor with whom I logged many hours in the air as well as considerable time in exotic places and on handball courts. We both went to Stanford, got degrees in aeronautical engineering, and our senses of humor meshed.

I'm indebted to another old friend, Tony Turpin, a renowned Pacific Northwest artist in various media, a retired navy captain, and a man with enormous intellect. He helped me add new twists to the manuscript and added many beneficial suggestions. He and I share many sea stories.

I owe a lot to my fellow pilot and good friend, Del Lubash. We flew together often, kept each other alive, and played golf hundreds of times with a net wager exchange of about five bucks over many years. Another close friend and fellow aviator, Jed Casey, reminded me of experiences from our squadrons at Whidbey Island, Washington. He also tried in vain to introduce me to the world of radio-controlled model airplane flying. I had trouble controlling the aircraft as it came toward me; I was too used to being in the cockpit. Fellow pilot and fine friend Jim Heemstra gave me a good briefing about flying from Berlin before I went there. He had some experience at that domicile and briefed me well on what to expect. Finally, another pilot and longtime friend, Tom Knepell, experienced with me many of the navy episodes I described. Our families lived together in Japan and remain close today.

All these folks gave beneficial suggestions and helped flesh out this book.

ABOUT THE AUTHOR

BILL SIREN LIVES IN San Diego with his wife, Allison, and near his children and grandchildren. He's a retired navy captain and spent several years as an international airline pilot. He's a graduate of Stanford University with advanced degrees in aeronautical engineering and business administration. He's also an alumnus of the National Defense University.

Bill flew eighty combat missions over Vietnam and served at the Pentagon for six years. He authored articles that have appeared in aviation journals and is a member of Beta Gamma Sigma and Tau Beta Pi, national honor societies in business and engineering respectively.